Important: Do not remove this
date due reminder.

DATE DUE

THE LIBRARY STORE   #47-0205

BY WHOSE HAND

Other books by Sandra Carey Cody

Consider the Lilly
Put Out the Light

BY WHOSE HAND

•

Sandra Carey Cody

AVALON BOOKS
NEW YORK

Published by Thomas Bouregy & Co., Inc.
160 Madison Avenue, New York, NY 10016

Library of Congress Cataloging-in-Publication Data

Cody, Sandra Carey.
    By whose hand / Sandra Carey Cody.
       p. cm.
    ISBN 978-0-8034-9948-5 (hardcover : acid-free paper)
    I. Title.

PS3603.O296B9 2009
813'.6—dc22

                                        2008048222

PRINTED IN THE UNITED STATES OF AMERICA
ON ACID-FREE PAPER
BY HADDON CRAFTSMEN, BLOOMSBURG, PENNSYLVANIA

To friends who inspire: Bob and Vicky Dombroski, Kate and Bert Elliott, Kay and Bard Haerland, Peter and Lydia LaPatourel—and, of course, Pete.

A special thanks to everyone I've had the pleasure of working with at Avalon Books. A lot of things change, but these folks remain helpful and accessible. Another thanks to Russ Durbin, who helped me figure out what kind of car a kid like Web Barrons would drive.

Chapter One

Jennie looked around the Peabody's sumptuous lobby, disregarded the sloppily dressed tourists, and focused on the couple seated on a leather sofa near the bar.

Leda and Preston Barrons occupied their chosen spot like royalty, sipping their drinks, oblivious to the masses. She knew the exact moment they spotted her. Preston rose and tilted his head in chivalrous greeting. Leda remained seated, sending the merest hint of a smile in Jennie's direction.

"Hi," Jennie said when she was close enough to be heard above the babble. She turned her cheek for Preston's chaste buss, then seated herself in a chair placed at a right angle to the sofa and waited for an explanation for the summons. And she had no doubt it was a summons. It wasn't every day she was invited to join the boss and her husband for cocktails at the South's most elegant hotel.

Leda's only response was another tight smile.

Preston glanced at his wife, moved a step closer to

her, and placed one hand on her shoulder but remained standing.

To Jennie, they looked worried. She wondered why, then decided she must be transferring her own unease. *What could the golden couple have to worry about? They should be glowing after the success of last weekend's Gala.*

Preston smiled at Jennie. "I'll get you a drink. What'll it be?"

"Just a ginger ale."

He strode off toward the bar.

Leda picked up her martini. The tinkle of ice in the glass sounded more than routine.

Jennie looked more closely. No question about it— Leda's hand was shaking. Leda, the iron matron, the terror of Riverview Manor, was a basket case this afternoon. The tension was too obvious to ignore. "Something wrong?" Jennie asked.

Leda nodded.

Preston returned with Jennie's ginger ale and took a seat next to his wife.

Jennie sipped her drink and tried to assess the situation. Preston patted Leda's hand. "We'll get through this."

Jennie studied them. They looked the epitome of the American Dream. Neither had been gifted with better than average looks, but they'd overcome that deficit by judicious use of two inherited fortunes. Their clothes were custom-made, their coiffures the handiwork of experts. Both sported enviable golf tans. Preston had the grace of a natural athlete. He was of medium height, trim and fit though no longer young. Jennie guessed him to be somewhere in his sixties. Leda, younger than her husband by almost twenty years, had a short, barrel-shaped torso that spoke more of resolve than grace, but she exuded that elusive quality known as presence, at least most of the time. Today . . .

She's nervous. Jennie figured it must have something to do with her. Otherwise why had she been summoned? Had she violated one of Leda's ironclad protocols? *Maybe Nate had done something.* That was always a possibility. Nathaniel Pynchon was Riverview Manor's chief troublemaker, and, as his major protector, Jennie took a lot of heat.

She switched her gaze to Preston, hoping for a clue from him.

None was forthcoming. Both Barronses seemed embarrassed by her presence. *They did invite me. They must've had a reason.* Should she ask? She took a deep breath and plunged. "I get the feeling you have something to tell me."

Leda's mouth remained compressed in a tight knot.

Must be serious. "Have I done something?" She was relieved to hear the words come out firmly and clearly.

Neither answered. Instead, they looked at each other, intensifying Jennie's discomfort.

John Philip Sousa's "King Cotton March" announced that it was time for the famous Peabody Hotel ducks to begin their ceremonious, twice-daily strut down the red carpet. Camera flashes went off in the background like heat lightning. The crowd in the lobby edged closer to the fountain.

Jennie, who'd been enthralled by the ritual since she was four years old, didn't even notice. "Are you going to ask me to leave Riverview?" There, she'd said it, voiced her worst fear. Next to her sons, Tommy and Andy, her job as Activities Director at Riverview Manor was the joy of her life. Not exactly a rose with no thorns but, nevertheless, a bloom to be treasured.

"Oh, my dear, no."

Jennie almost dropped her drink. Leda was not a demonstrative person, especially with employees. To be called "my dear" by her was unsettling, to say the least.

"Look," Jennie said, "something's obviously wrong. How about we just lay it out?"

Instead of answering, Leda stared at the crowds milling around the travertine marble fountain.

Preston looked toward the bar, shook his head, and squared his shoulders as though he'd come to a decision. "You're right," he said. He paused and looked at his wife before he continued. "Something is very wrong."

Leda made a visible effort to compose herself. She stretched her short torso to its full height and looked Jennie in the eye for the first time since she'd joined them. "The money raised at the Gala has disappeared."

"I don't understand."

Leda looked over Jennie's head, toward the crowd leaning over the iron railing of the mezzanine. "Neither do we."

Preston put a hand on his wife's arm. "Actually, 'disappeared' isn't quite accurate."—he paused to clear his throat—"what we mean is, it's gone from Riverview's account."

Jennie's cheeks began to burn. *Why tell me?* She remembered the events following Riverview's annual benefit on Saturday night, a little over a week ago now. She spoke slowly, careful to get the sequence exactly right. "I gave the money to . . . I don't remember his name . . . that guy from your bank. Tall, thin."

Preston prompted her. "Rob Payton?"

"Yes. Anyway, he counted the cash. There wasn't much. It was mostly checks. He tallied everything. I verified it. We made sure we had copies of receipts we'd given for cash donations. I xeroxed the checks. He filled out a deposit slip. We compared total receipts and check copies with the amount of the deposit. When we were sure it was right, he put everything into one of those lock bags and took it with him."

Both Leda and Preston were leaning forward, intent on every word.

He said, "Yes, we know all that. The money was deposited into Riverview's Special Account. I checked Monday morning. The amount matched the copy of the deposit receipt."

"Then what—"

He went on. "Forty-eight hours later, it was gone."

Jennie still didn't understand. "Can't you trace it? There's always a trail, especially now, with computers."

Leda spoke this time. "That's the problem. The money has been traced. It turned up in Web's account."

"Web? Your son?" Jennie knew how dumb she sounded. How many Webs did she know? Who except her son could reduce the formidable Leda Barrons to Jell-O? And what could it possibly have to do with her? Only one way to find out. "Why are you telling me this?"

Leda opened her mouth.

Preston stopped her with a hand on her arm. "We're hoping you can help." He brought his other hand out of his pocket with a movement evocative of a magician and placed an object on the parquet table beside Jennie's chair.

A key lay there—ordinary yet out of place.

Jennie folded her hands in her lap, as far from the foreign object as she could manage. "Help?"

Preston said, "I *know* my son did not take the money." His eyes met Jennie's, daring her to disagree. "I also know there's evidence in the building to prove his innocence."

" 'Building'? You mean Riverview?"

"No, the bank."

"How can you be sure?"

"It had to be someone in the firm who made the transfer."

Leda interrupted now. She reached out to stroke her husband's arm, then turned to Jennie. "Do you know what it cost Preston to say that?"

"Yes." Jennie's response was quick. Everyone knew of Preston Barrons' pride in the bank founded by his great-grandfather.

Preston smiled at his wife. "Painful or not, it's obvious someone who works for me took money from Riverview's Special Account and transferred it to our son's account. They used his laptop to make the transfer."

Jennie tried to make sense of it. "Maybe one of his friends did it. A practical joke gone bad?"

"No. Web's working for me at the bank this summer. He's not in the habit of taking work home at night. Nor his computer. It had to be someone in the bank."

Jennie asked, "How did you find out where the money was?"

"It was fairly simple. Both accounts are in-house."

" 'In-house'?"

"Both are held in my bank. Our IT person followed the trail in no time."

"But whoever transferred the money must have known it would be easy to trace. If they knew enough to figure out the codes . . . There are codes, aren't there?"

"Of course," Preston said.

Jennie went on. "They had to know that someone else could figure out what they'd done."

"Exactly!" Preston slapped his knee.

Leda beamed approval at Jennie.

"You're saying they wanted the transfer traced?" Jennie was working it out as she spoke.

Leda's head bobbed like a dashboard ornament. "It's a deliberate attempt to frame Web."

"Any idea why?"

Preston said, "This is speculation, of course, but I'm pretty sure it's correct. My sixty-fifth birthday is coming up. Everyone's wondering if I plan to retire. More to the point, they wonder whom I'll appoint as my successor."

Leda said, "Someone wants to make sure it isn't Web."

"But Web's only . . . what? Twenty?"

Both nodded.

"So . . . is he really old enough to be a threat?"

Preston hunched his shoulders. "If they discredit my son, the Board might ask me to retire. Then, even when Web is older, he won't have a chance."

"Can they do that?"

"They can't force me"—Preston paused to gulp the rest of his drink—"but they can certainly make it uncomfortable. Rumors could be leaked to the press."

"Rumors? Like what?"

"Wouldn't have to be anything specific. Hints of shady dealings, innuendoes too small to deny, just enough to cast doubt on my integrity."

"Who would do that?"

Leda and Preston exchanged quick glances, but neither answered.

Jennie resisted the urge to fill the quiet. She sipped her drink and waited, wondering what they wanted from her.

Leda must have read her mind. "We're asking you to help us find out."

"How? I'm not a computer expert. Isn't that the kind of person you need?"

Leda placed both small hands in her lap and leaned forward. Her manicured fingertips looked like drops of blood on the white linen skirt. "No."

Preston said, "That's exactly what we don't need. I know the evidence is in the building, probably on the sixth floor, but it's not on any of the computers." He tapped the key lying on the table with one long, tapered finger. His nails were as expertly cared for as his wife's. "There has to be something that will lead us to whoever took the money."

Jennie was doubtful. "Wouldn't they be careful not to leave anything like that lying around?"

"Under normal circumstances, yes." Preston placed his glass on the table. "I discovered the theft late Wednesday and stewed about it overnight and half of Thursday. Then, just before noon on Thursday, I announced a bonus holiday for everyone on the sixth floor."

Jennie didn't understand. "Just the sixth floor?"

Preston clarified for her. "That's where the employees closest to me work. I made a joke about how they'd better leave before I changed my mind. Then I shooed them out. Told them not to come back until Monday. No one had time to clean up his or her work area."

"Didn't the rest of the bank wonder about that?"

Preston shrugged, the gesture of a man not accustomed to justifying his actions, especially to employees.

Jennie wondered where this was going. "Since the bank was still open, how do you know no one came back?"

"Actually, that was my plan. I made a show of leaving with everyone else. Then I returned and waited. Figured anyone with something to hide would show up. No one did."

"They had Thursday and Friday nights and all day Saturday."

"I'm confident no one went back." Preston scowled and glanced toward the bar. It was clear he was losing patience. He retrieved the key from the center of the table and held it toward Jennie. "I want you to use this to go to the sixth-floor offices and look around."

"You mean now? Sunday evening, when no one's there?"

"Tonight would be better. Very late." He pressed the key into her hand. "Only a few people know enough about the system to make the transfer. The work space of everyone with access to the kind of information we're talking about is located near my office." He reached into the inner breast pocket of his impeccably tailored blazer, brought out a folded sheet of lined yellow paper, and handed it to Jennie. "Here's a diagram of the area." There was absolute confidence in his every movement. Apparently it hadn't occurred to him that Jennie would say no.

She tried to think of a way to set him straight without antagonizing Leda. She lay the key on the table, smoothed the paper, and saw a series of neat boxes, each with a name printed in it. To buy time, she asked, "What about security?"

"Here's the guard's schedule." Preston handed over another paper. "You don't have to worry about being interrupted."

"Cleaning people?"

"I left special instructions for the sixth floor to be left alone until after-hours Monday. Staff arrives at eight-thirty. If you check the schedule, you'll see that the guard won't be on that floor until nearly five." He picked up the key. "There's a side door, opening into the stairwell, and, from there, a door into the lobby. This key fits both. Take the elevator to the sixth floor. If you go around 2:00 A.M., you'll have plenty of time to poke around these offices without interruption."

"What if I do get interrupted? What if I get arrested for breaking and entering?"

Preston chuckled. "How can you? I own the building, and I'm giving you the key so you can retrieve some papers for me. It's that simple."

"Then why don't you do it yourself?"

He looked embarrassed. "Actually, I tried, but I couldn't find anything." He glanced at his wife.

Leda said, "It was my idea to ask you. You seem to have a knack for unraveling plots."

A knack you never approved of before. Jennie refrained

from pointing this out and contented herself with, "Why not the police?"

"Since the money showed up in Web's account . . ." Leda let her voice drift and looked at Jennie with pleading eyes. "You're a mother. Surely you can understand that we want to protect our son."

Jennie looked at Preston. "Aren't you supposed to report things like this?"

"As soon as Web is cleared, we'll go to the authorities."

"The IT guy who traced the transfer—won't he report it?"

"That's another reason for finding evidence before the business day starts tomorrow."

"I sympathize with you, but I can't—"

Preston interrupted. "You realize I have to freeze all expenditures from the trust until this is cleared up."

" 'Freeze expenditures'?" Jennie stared at him, trying to force him to speak the threat aloud. He didn't, so she did. "My salary comes from trust income."

He met her gaze without flinching.

"So I won't get paid." Mentally, she calculated how long her savings would last. Not long. She sat back, considering her options.

Preston said, "Unfortunately that's true, but I'm sure you understand that my first duty is to protect the trust's assets."

Leda spoke again. "Jennie, please. We realize what we're asking is unorthodox, but it's all for the good of Riverview."

Riverview, my ankle. It's for the good of the Barrons

family. Jennie left this thought unspoken. She knew that, in Leda's mind, anything that affected the Barrons family affected Riverview, an opinion she had to admit was not totally unwarranted.

Chapter Two

Jennie slathered peanut butter onto a piece of bread, folded it in half, and poured a glass of milk, all the while questioning her judgment in agreeing to sneak into the bank in the middle of the night. *Am I being stupid?* Only one answer to that—a resounding *yes!* She could always find another job. She knew that's what she should do. Preston Barrons needed to be shown there was someone he couldn't bully.

She looked at her cell phone, lying on the table beside her bank statement. She picked it up, set it back down. How could she leave Riverview? Being Activities Director at the retirement facility was more than a job. Leaving Riverview meant leaving the residents—Nate, Georgie, Doreen, Tess, and all the others—people almost as dear to her as her own family. There had to be another way. She contemplated calling Preston and asking him to go with her. *Then, if I get caught, there's no question I have a right to be there.* It seemed such a natural solution, she

13

wondered why she hadn't suggested it earlier—or why he hadn't thought of it himself.

The telephone rang.

That could be him now. Maybe he had the same idea. Optimistic, she picked up the receiver. "Hello."

"Hey, Jen." Her ex-husband, Tom's, baritone came through, with the excited babble of two young boys in the background. "Thought we'd better call and see how you're doing back there all by yourself."

This was even better—the kids calling for one last "Love ya" before they headed farther out into the wilderness. "I'm fine. Where are you guys?"

"Williams, Arizona. We spent the day at the Grand Canyon. Walked partway down."

"How'd they like it?"

"I'll let them tell you. Here's Andy."

There were sounds of the phone being handed off, followed by a "Mom!" that could only belong to an over-stimulated seven-year-old.

"Hey, Andy. How ya doin'?"

"Great. We saw the Grand Canyon today."

"What do you think of it?"

"It's huge. Even bigger than I thought. Did you get our postcards?"

"Not yet. When'd you send them?"

"Couple days ago. From Oklahoma City."

"Did you have fun with your cousins?"

"Uh-huh. We went to the Old West Museum."

"That sounds interesting."

"Yeah, it was. That's where I got my postcard."

"Can't wait to see it."

There were sounds of the phone being wrestled away.

"You there, Mom?" Tommy's voice now. He was two years older than his brother and, at least by his own estimation, light-years more mature.

"Yep, I'm still here. So, you finally got to see that big hole you've been reading about?"

"Yeah. And we saw the mules that take people down to the bottom. But you have to be taller than us. Dad said maybe in a couple of years."

She talked to Tommy for a few more minutes, then Andy, telling them both that she loved them and hoped they had a great time. Andy said, "Dad wants to talk to you again."

Tom came back on. "We won't be calling for a few days. But they'll be okay. We'll only get in touch if there's an emergency. Keep that in mind when you don't hear from us."

Something in his manner, his assumption that she had no life without him and the kids, made her say, "Don't worry about me. I have my own little adventure lined up."

"Oh?"

She gave herself a mental kick and tried to make light of her remark. "It's kind of funny, really. Preston Barrons asked me to go to his bank tonight and retrieve some papers. Very cloak-and-dagger."

"You're kidding, right?"

" 'Fraid not." She gave him a quick version of the story Leda and Preston had told her, ending with, "So, I don't have much choice. Either I help them out, or I don't get paid. Anyway, there's nothing illegal about it. Preston gave me the key."

"Maybe Web actually did make the transfer. Have you thought about that? The kid's not exactly an Eagle Scout."

"He wouldn't do anything that stupid."

"He's no Einstein either."

"Everybody deserves the benefit of the doubt."

"Why you? They can afford a professional."

"I've figured out some knotty problems for Riverview before. Leda knows that. And she wants to keep it in the family, so to speak."

"You're being naïve."

Though Jennie and Tom were no longer married, he still had the infuriating habit of assuming that he knew what was best for her. She started to argue but bit her tongue because she knew their sons were close by, listening. She kept her tone mild and said, "Don't worry about me. You just concentrate on keeping the kids safe. I'm not taking any chances."

She talked to each of the boys one more time before they said their good-byes, then settled in to wait. She repeated to herself her last statement to Tom: "I'm not taking any chances." *Am I? Can anything go wrong? Well, sure, things can always go wrong, but how bad can it be? A little embarrassment maybe. Nothing a phone call won't straighten out.*

She nibbled the edge of the peanut butter sandwich— dried out and unappetizing now. The milk was lukewarm, equally unappetizing. She discarded both and headed for the family room, seeking diversion. She clicked the TV remote, searching for something, anything, to keep her imagination from running rampant.

The screen flickered to life. No. She wasn't in the mood for baseball.

Click. Even less for NASCAR.

Another *click.* An elegant black-and-white image held her attention, and she settled deeper into the chair, trusting Lauren Bacall and Humphrey Bogart to distract her from the doubts swirling in her head.

Chapter Three

J ennie held her breath and fitted the key into the lock. It clicked and turned easily. First hurdle cleared. She swung the heavy metal door outward, stepped into the small area at the foot of a stairwell, and allowed the door to close behind her. The air was sour and swelteringly hot. A bare yellow bulb mounted at the turning of the stairs cast an oppressive wash on dull green walls.

Directly opposite the side entrance was a door leading to the main lobby, just as Preston had described it. She twisted the knob and was surprised when it yielded without her using the key. Preston had said the key fit both locks. *Did someone forget to lock the second door?* She opened the door partway and peered through the six-inch crack. A welcome blast of air-conditioning cooled her cheeks.

The bank lobby seemed a different world at night, illuminated only by dim emergency spots that shone from the ceiling onto the cotton-blossom design inlaid into the marble floor. Mahogany-paneled walls and equally somber furnishings absorbed whatever illumination made its way to the outer edges of the space. Jennie squinted past the massive desks toward the wall on the left. Brass scrollwork fashioned into a series of cotton blossoms protected the glass elevator doors. Its polished sheen reflected just enough rays to seem threatening. She glanced at her watch. 2:08. *The guard should be in the basement now.* She stepped through the door, made a tentative move toward the elevator, then stopped. *What if he notices the floor indicator above the elevator?* She was pretty sure Preston hadn't thought of that. *He's never had to sneak in. He owns the place.*

She closed the door and started up the stairs. It didn't hurt to be careful. Who knew how religiously the guard followed his schedule? At the top of the third flight, she stopped for a breather. *Halfway there.* A line of smudged handprints stained the wall above the railing, the only indication that another human had ever been in the space.

Jennie adjusted the small backpack she'd brought in lieu of a purse. Her T-shirt, drenched with perspiration, clung to her skin. Her jeans felt as if they were constructed of iron. The higher she climbed, the hotter the air was— like a reverse descent into hell. When she reached the door with a 6 stenciled on it, she leaned against the metal surface and took a series of deep breaths. She looked at her watch again. 2:11. She fished the schedule Preston had given her out of her pocket and held the paper so the light shone on it. *Guard should be checking first floor outside doors.* She turned to face the entry to the sixth floor. *It's now or never.*

She twisted the knob and stepped into the carpeted

area that held the work spaces of Preston Barrons and the employees closest to him. The offices she'd been told to concentrate on were along the wall opposite her: Rob Payton, Preston's second-in-command, occupied the right corner; next was the office of Karl Erickson, Rob's assistant; after that, a conference room; then Charlotte Ellio, Preston's administrative assistant. Preston's office was in the left corner, last in the lineup, twice as large as any of the others. It was the only one with the door closed. Jennie wondered if it was locked. *Doesn't matter. He said not to bother with his office.* Desks, arranged in neat rows, occupied the open area between her and the wall of offices. The scant light disappeared into the thick pile of the carpet, relieving the darkness just enough for her to see a path through the aisles of desks.

She rummaged in her backpack until she located the penlight she'd brought, then headed across the room toward Rob Payton's office. With Web out of the way, he was Preston's logical successor. He knew more about the bank's operation than anyone except Preston. *Besides, he's just a little too—What?* She tried to pinpoint the reason for her dislike of the man as she switched the flashlight on and approached his desk.

She directed the beam over its surface, which was mostly clear, with three framed photographs ranged along the back edge and a tidy pile of paper on the front right corner. She looked first at the pictures: a girl who appeared to be in her early teens, sitting in the grass with her arms around a pair of schnauzers; Rob and an athletic-looking woman Jennie recognized as his wife, Margaret, seated on a golf cart; Rob and Margaret, standing next to Preston and Leda Barrons, all of them dressed in formal attire. Typical family stuff, with a photo of the boss and his wife thrown in to polish the apple.

Jennie sat in the black leather swivel chair and pulled the stack of papers to the center of the desk. She scanned the top sheet—rows and rows of numbers that meant nothing to her. Next in the pile, same thing, equally meaningless. She used her chin to hold the penlight steady while she flipped through the papers. More of the same. At this point, what she wanted most was to get out of there, something that would take forever working in the dark. She hesitated a few seconds, switched on the desk lamp, then ducked when its light flooded onto the desktop. Crouched behind the desk, she listened, half expecting to hear someone yell, "Who's there?" No one did. *I heard something, though. Almost like . . . No, it's probably just the air-conditioning. All buildings have noises.* She became conscious of a dull pain in her hand, looked down, and realized she had a death grip on a drawer pull. She released it and flexed her fingers. *The guard's still on the first floor. Anyway, what's he gonna do? Shoot first, ask questions later?*

She looked through the stack of papers again: lots of figures, a list of names with phone numbers beside them. A small scrap near the bottom caught her attention. On it was written a single figure: $68,750. *That's the amount raised by the Gala.* She stared at it. *Makes sense for him to have that. He counted the money with me. Anyway, Preston must've seen it when he searched the offices himself. This is a waste of time. I don't even know what I'm looking for. Well, I'm here. May as well go ahead.*

She turned her attention to the wastebasket. Not much

there—just half a dozen folded sheets of paper. She scooped them out and placed them on the desk before her. Next, she opened the center drawer and tore a sheet off a three-inch-square pad of Post-its. As she started to write, she noticed dark streaks on the paper. She checked her hands; her fingertips were blackened. She rubbed them together. The substance came off easily. She sniffed her fingers. *Ashes.* She directed the penlight beam to the bottom of the trash can and saw scraps of burned paper. *This could be it.* She found an envelope in a side drawer and placed the charred bits in it, careful to keep them intact. She placed the envelope along the most rigid surface in her backpack. Then she turned her attention again to the Post-it, wrote *from R. Payton's wastebasket* on it, secured the whole thing with a paper clip, and slipped it into the backpack. *I'll check these out later.* With this decision made, she turned off the lamp and moved on to the next office.

This belongs to—she closed her eyes to summon up a picture of the diagram Preston had drawn for her—*Karl Erickson. He's Rob's assistant. There's a good chance he'd know if Rob were up to anything.*

Erickson was nowhere near as neat as his boss. His desktop was hardly visible beneath the clutter of disarranged papers. This time Jennie skipped the obvious and shone the flashlight into the wastebasket first. A sour, ciderish smell wafted up. *Lot of possibilities in this mess.* The trash can was almost half full of wadded-up balls of paper. Jennie went with her earlier decision to take the contents home and study them later. The problem here was volume. Could she fit all this into her pack? She rummaged deeper. Her fingers touched something cold and damp. She jerked her hand out and checked with the flashlight. A half-eaten apple. Beneath the apple was a Lowenstein's bag. Jennie loaded the crumpled paper into the plastic department-store bag. She squeezed the packet, forcing out air and compacting the papers until it was a fourth its original size, then stuffed it into the backpack, pleased with herself that she'd thought to bring a practical container.

When she left Erickson's office, she stopped to peer into the conference room. *I don't think there'd be anything in there. I'll move on and come back if I have time.*

Charlotte Ellio, Preston's administrative assistant, occupied the next office. Her desktop held an upright file organizer, an in-and out-box, a dictionary, and a cup filled with assorted pens and pencils. A calendar pad covered the work surface in the center. Most of the squares were filled with tiny, meticulous printing. Jennie looked closer. *Preston's appointments.*

The wastebasket contained scraps of paper of varying sizes, plus a sheaf of folded newspaper. Jennie fished out the scraps and stuck them into her tote. She glanced at the newspapers. *Probably not worth worrying about.* She took another look before moving on and noticed that a number of items had been circled with a black pen. *They're important to somebody.* She stuffed the newspapers into an outside pocket of the backpack.

What was that?

Had she only imagined sounds coming from the office next door? She ran her thumb down the side of the penlight, turned the switch off, and crouched behind the desk.

There! Again!

Sounds too soft to be given a name but too distinct to be her imagination. A different sound, louder, higher pitched. Then nothing.

The harder she listened, the more silent the building seemed. The only noise she could be sure of was her own breathing.

She waited a minute or two that seemed like three days. Still no sound. She considered searching the conference room. *No. I'll do a quick check of the desks in the open area and split.* She paused at the office threshold to look around. Nothing alarming.

She headed for a desk just outside Preston's office.

Wait a minute. Wasn't his door closed?

She tried to picture the lineup of doors facing her when she'd stepped out of the stairwell.

I'm sure it was.

She leaned against the door frame.

Maybe a draft from the air conditioner blew it open. That could be what I heard.

She glanced at the overhead vent, weighing this possibility.

Drafts blow doors closed, not open.

She looked toward the elevator and realized that the arrow above the door was moving.

It's going down.

A shiver danced up her spine. Her heart was pounding. She forced slow, deep breaths and shifted her gaze to the office with the formerly closed door.

Somebody had been in Preston's office. The one he told me to leave alone.

She wondered, not for the first time, why he closed his door when the others were left open. Intuition told her that whatever she needed to find was in that room. Should she go in after it? Whatever *it* might be?

I've come too far to turn back now.

She pushed the door the rest of the way open without allowing herself to second-guess her resolve. The creaking she'd heard earlier repeated itself.

It's okay. They're gone now.

She moved forward. An odd smell brought her to a halt. It took her a minute to place the odor. *Summer picnics . . . fireworks!*

She looked toward the elevator. The arrow was motionless now, steady above the Roman numeral indicating the first floor. She shone the flashlight on the desktop. There were no papers in sight, no pictures, just a silver paperweight in the shape of a cotton boll. She turned back. Her foot struck something. She turned the flashlight on.

Its beam fell onto a pale yellow golf shirt, a tanned arm. The desk obscured the rest of the form.

She took more deep breaths, resisting the impulse to flee. Willing her hand to stop shaking, she dropped to one knee, reached for the wrist, tried to find a pulse. None. She rose but couldn't bring herself to walk around the desk and look at the face.

I'll get the guard.

In her rush to the door, she kicked something; it skittered across the floor and hit the wall with a thud. She directed the flashlight toward it. A gun. Short. Stubby. Like the one her father used for shooting targets at the range.

Chapter Four

Jennie closed the door to Preston Barrons' office behind her. The schedule she'd so recently checked was gone from her head. She passed Charlotte Ellio's door and went to the empty conference room. There, she pressed her forehead to the cool glass of a window and closed her eyes for a moment before she looked again at the crumpled paper. The guard wouldn't be on the sixth floor until nearly 3:00 A.M. She checked her watch. *Another twenty minutes. Can't wait. He should be on the fourth floor now.* She got into the elevator and pushed the button for 4.

Before the doors were completely open, an unfamiliar voice barked, "Hold it!" She glimpsed a stocky figure in dark clothing before a beam of light struck her in the face, blinding her.

She used a hand to shield her eyes but was unable to see past the glare. "Are you the security guard?"

"Never mind who I am. Who are you?"

"Jennie Connors. You have to call the police immediately."

"What're you doing here?"

"Preston Barrons sent me to look for something."

"Why would Mr. Barrons do that?"

"Please, just call the police."

The man moved closer. "I've seen you before."

"I work at Riverview Manor. I come into the bank sometimes with Mrs. Barrons."

He stepped closer, bringing the hand holding the light to within inches of her face. After an eternity he breathed "Ah" and switched off the beam. "What're you doing here at this time of night?"

"I told you. Preston Barrons asked me to look for something." When he didn't answer, she put a hand into her pocket, brought out the key, and dangled it before his eyes. "He gave me this. Look—*P. B.,* his initials."

He took the key ring from her and studied it.

"Look, Mr.—What's your name?"

He hesitated before answering. "Dan Norbill."

"Somebody's been shot up there, and whoever did it is getting farther away while you stand gaping at me."

"Shot?" The guard stepped back. His face registered a series of warring emotions. Skepticism finally won. "Show me."

Jennie returned to the elevator. Norbill followed. Neither spoke as the car swayed upward. When it lurched to a stop, he swung the flashlight forward, motioning her to exit first.

She stepped out, then moved aside and pointed toward the only office with its door closed. "Over there."

"Mr. Barrons' office?"

She nodded, grateful when he stalked off without waiting. Her thin T-shirt, still damp with perspiration, felt icy now against her skin. Her legs were shaking so badly, she could hardly stand. She eased herself down until she was sitting on the floor and leaned against a wall, hugging herself and shivering. From this position, she watched the door open and Norbill disappear into the room.

Light flooded out. There was a startled curse that made Jennie think the security guard was even less used to dealing with corpses than she was. She tried to relax, telling herself, *It's his problem now,* though she knew it was infinitely more complicated than that.

She watched the door until Norbill emerged, holding a cell phone to his ear. To Jennie, it looked as if he was doing more listening than talking. He paced back and forth, darting suspicious looks her way, shaking his head. He finished with a final emphatic nod, lowered the phone, and strode toward her.

She forced her eyes to meet his.

He turned away and made another call. Then he closed the phone and shoved it into the carrier strapped to his belt. He approached Jennie and said, "Come with me."

When she rose from her place on the floor, he led her to the conference room, directed her to a chair at the far end of the table, and said, "Mr. Barrons will be here shortly. Don't talk to anyone 'til he gets here."

"Did you call the police?"

"Yes." He started to leave.

"Wait."

He stopped, then stood with his legs wide apart, slapping the flashlight into his palm.

"Do you know who it is? Who got shot, I mean?"

"Mr. Payton."

"Rob Payton?"

"Yeah." He turned and trotted toward the elevator without giving Jennie a chance to ask for more detail.

The room was semidark, with the only light coming from emergency spots in the ceiling. Jennie sat at the conference table, put her elbows on the burnished teak surface, closed her eyes, and massaged her temples while she struggled to make sense of the night's events. So Rob Payton was dead now. Why? Because of the stolen funds? What had he been doing in his boss's office? *No use.* It was like trying to solve a cryptogram in an unfamiliar language. Within minutes she heard a siren, low at first, then growing louder. She waited, watching the elevator door, and was both relieved and apprehensive when it opened.

Norbill exited first, followed by two uniformed police officers. They spoke in tones so low, their words were indistinguishable to Jennie. Norbill led the way to the large corner office, two doors from where she waited.

She squared her shoulders, attempting to compose herself. She'd have to face them soon. *Please, please don't make me go back in there.* Muffled sounds from the office suggested people bumping into furniture. Jennie pictured them moving around the room, careful not to disturb the body. She sat rigid and clasped her hands in her lap, trying to block the image. She picked at a torn cuticle until it began to bleed. Holding the hand with the bloody thumb aloft, she used the other to dig through her backpack. She reached deep, past the papers she'd gleaned from the wastebaskets, and kept going until she located a small packet of tissues.

One of the uniformed policemen appeared in the door-way. "You Jennie Connors?"

"Yes." She wrapped a tissue around her finger and braced herself for his questions.

None came. Not yet. She knew it was just a matter of time.

The man looked around the room. "Stay put, you hear?"

"Okay."

He nodded, then left without speaking again.

Jennie could see only the area between the row of offices and the elevator. She could hear but not see the activity in Preston's office. She watched Norbill cross the space, enter the elevator, and disappear. He reappeared a few minutes later with more men. Jennie watched them look under desks and check the room's corners. Occasionally one of the men glanced her way, but mostly they ignored her.

The elevator doors parted again, and Preston Barrons stepped out. Here, at last, was a familiar face. Jennie sent up a silent thanks. Guilt prompted her to add another prayer, this time for the lifeless form of Rob Payton lying just two doors away. She thought of the pictures she'd seen on his desk: his wife, his young daughter—laughing, innocent, and happy, playing with her dogs. *They'll be getting a phone call. Maybe right now.* She shied away from thinking about that.

After the initial relief of seeing Preston, Jennie's brain registered that he was not alone. She looked at his companion and recognized Hamilton Sunderson, the Barronses' attorney. She knew Sunderson, since he also represented Riverview. He was an imposing figure, distinguished-looking in the way some men are when they reach their fifties. Even at this hour, when he must have been dragged from his bed, he looked poised and imperturbable. He was tall—six foot three, maybe four—with classic Nordic features, graying hair perfectly cut, and blue eyes that gave no clue that anything might be amiss. His clothing—tan linen slacks and a sage green button-down shirt—looked magazine-ad perfect,

Preston Barrons, on the other hand, was rumpled and puffy-eyed, a far cry from the urbane presence who'd smooth-talked Jennie into searching the bank offices for him.

The two recent arrivals stopped to speak with one of the policemen before they joined Jennie in the conference room. Preston entered first. Sunderson followed him in and closed the door.

Preston lay a hand on Jennie's shoulder. "You okay?"

"Okay as can be expected, I guess."

Sunderson interrupted. "Let's get on with it." He maneuvered Barrons out of the way and stood in front of Jennie. "What happened?"

Barrons answered before she had a chance to respond. "She was looking for something for me. She used my key to get in and had my permission to be here."

"You already told me that. I need to hear from her exactly what transpired."

"I don't want her to get into trouble for this."

Jennie spoke up. "I have a feeling I'm already in trouble. I just want to tell the police what happened and go home."

"Tell me first"—Sunderson smiled for the first time, a

dazzling exhibition of teeth and charm—"and we'll get you out of here as soon as we can."

There was a knock on the door. A disembodied voice penetrated the heavy wood. "We're ready to talk to Mrs. Connors."

"In a minute." Sunderson's low voice carried the privileged inflections of the Old South and sent a clear message that he was not intimidated. His gaze remained fixed on Jennie. "Tell me exactly what happened."

She recapped her journey up the stairs, her exploration of the offices, the noises she'd heard, her discovery of the body.

Sunderson said, "Did you find anything in the offices?"

"You know what I found."

"I mean, anything about the money?"

Preston leaned forward at the last question.

"No."

"And you didn't see another person?"

"No, but I know I didn't miss him by—"

" 'Him'? How do you know it was a man?"

She took a minute to think. "Actually, I don't. It could have been a woman. I only heard the door squeak when . . . someone . . . left Preston's office. I hid behind the desk a few minutes. Didn't come out until I was pretty sure they weren't coming back. I noticed Preston's office door was open. Right after that, I realized the elevator was moving."

"Why did you go into Mr. Barrons' office? My understanding is that you were instructed not to."

What kind of question is that? Jennie wondered what Sunderson was getting at but confined her answer to: "Because when I saw the door open—I was pretty sure it had been closed when I got here—I knew someone had been in there. I figured they'd just gone down in the elevator, and I went to check."

Another knock sounded. Louder this time.

Over his shoulder, Sunderson said, "One more minute." His eyes remained focused on Jennie. "You ready?"

She nodded.

"Okay. Keep your answers short. Tell the truth, but don't volunteer anything."

"I don't have anything to hide."

"Did I ask you to hide anything?" The attorney didn't wait for an answer; he went to the door and put his hand on the knob.

Jennie stopped him. "Wait a minute. I have a couple of questions myself before I talk to the police." She leaned toward Preston Barrons. "Did you know what I was going to find when you asked me to come here?"

"Of course not!"

"Why didn't you come with me?"

He didn't answer; he merely compressed his mouth into a tight line that made his lips disappear.

Sunderson interceded, smooth as silk. "There's time to go into that later. Right now, we have to let them in." He inclined his head toward the door. To Jennie, he said, "Just tell them what you told me. No more. No less. And don't be nervous. There's no need."

Preston added, "We won't let anything bad happen to you."

Yeah, right!

Chapter Five

When Sunderson opened the door, a short, burly man shuffled in. He glanced at the three people in the room. His eyes narrowed when he saw Jennie, but he didn't comment, didn't acknowledge that he knew her. As if directed by a special cop's radar, he zeroed in on the lawyer and flashed a badge. "Lieutenant Stanley Masoski, Homicide, Memphis Police."

"I'm Hamilton Sunderson, an attorney representing Barrons Bank and Trust Company." He stepped forward when he spoke, taking advantage of his height to look down on the policeman. There were a couple of seconds while the two men sized each other up, two animals circling each other without actually moving.

Sunderson spoke first. He looked toward Jennie. "This is—"

Masoski interrupted. "Mrs. Connors and I have met. Lady has a habit of being in the wrong place at the wrong time." With that, he turned away from Sunderson and Barrons and focused on Jennie, skipping any niceties. "Okay, let's hear it. How did you come to discover the body?"

Preston answered for her. "She's here at my request."

"You're . . . ?"

"Preston Barrons." He drew himself up and lifted his chin. "I own the building. My family founded this bank. I gave Jennifer the key and asked her to check something for me."

"At"—Masoski looked at his watch—"three o'clock in the morning?"

"I don't know why the time is relevant."

"Maybe it's not," Masoski said. His expression was bland, his tone mild.

Jennie had seen that mildness before and knew how deceptive it was. She wanted to warn Preston not to underestimate this particular cop—not that she was worried about him. She figured he could take care of himself. She was the one who'd be caught in the middle.

Sunderson positioned himself between his client and Masoski. "You're both right," he said. His tone was conciliatory. "The time itself is not what's relevant here." He tilted his head toward Barrons. "But you'll have to agree, Preston, it is unusual to ask a young woman to enter a banking facility in the middle of the night." Then he turned and favored Masoski with his million-dollar smile. "We have a rather complicated situation here. Let's sit down and discuss it."

Jennie knew Masoski well enough to read distrust and just a touch of amusement in his eyes, but he complied with the suggestion to sit. He chose a chair at the far end of the table, where he had an unobstructed view of the activity in the area outside the conference room.

Preston and Sunderson sat side by side, across the table from Jennie.

Masoski removed a small spiral notebook from his shirt pocket and looked at Jennie. "First, I want to know how you discovered the body. Start with your entry into the building. I want times, places, anything, anyone, you saw or heard."

Jennie was aware that both Preston Barrons and Hamilton Sunderson were watching her, but she ignored them. "I used the key Mr. Barrons gave me and came in through the side entrance."

Sunderson shifted in his chair but said nothing.

Masoski said, "When did he give you this key?"

"This afternoon. Well, actually, yesterday afternoon. It was sometime between four and five o'clock Sunday. He and his wife invited me for a drink at the Peabody, and—"

Preston interrupted. "So, you see, Lieutenant, there was nothing clandestine about our meeting. Everyone in Memphis could have—"

Sunderson put a hand on his client's arm.

Preston darted a quick look at the lawyer, then became quiet.

Masoski nodded encouragingly at Jennie.

She continued. "Anyway, I used the key to get in. I didn't want to alert the guard, so I took the stairs up."

"If you had Mr. Barrons' permission to be here, why avoid the guard?"

She hesitated, hoping Preston would come to her aid. He had, after all, given her the schedule. Why would she need to know where the guard was other than to avoid him? When Preston remained silent, she said, "I'm not

sure, actually. I guess I just didn't want to get into any involved explanations." Masoski didn't comment, so she
went on. "I was looking through the offices. When I
started to leave, I noticed that Mr. Barrons' door was open.
I was pretty sure it had been closed when I got off the elevator. I went to check and . . ." She faltered, swallowing
hard.

"And what?"

"I saw someone lying on the floor."

"Someone? Didn't you recognize the person?"

"Actually, I only saw the arm. I checked for a pulse,
and when I didn't find one, I went looking for the guard.
When I—"

Masoski interrupted. "Why look for the guard? Why
didn't you call the police immediately?"

"I don't know." She paused, thought a minute. "I think I
just needed to be with someone. Someone alive, I mean."
Her hands were shaking. She put them into her lap, held
them steady between her knees, and looked Masoski in
the eye. "Anyway, as soon I found the guard, I asked him
to call the police."

No one in the room spoke.

Jennie said, "I didn't know it was Rob Payton until the
guard told me."

"Did you know Mr. Payton before?"

"I'd met him. I didn't really know him."

Preston said, "Rob Payton was my employee. Jennifer
met him when my bank sponsored a fund-raiser for
Riverview Manor. That's where she works. The two of
them counted the money and made up the deposit." His
voice betrayed no emotion.

Jennie looked at him, searching for something, anything, in his face. It was impassive.

Masoski gave both of them a hard look, then said to Jennie, "The guard says he stopped you coming down in the elevator, trying to leave the building."

"That's not true. I knew he'd be on the fourth floor, and I took the elevator to get to him."

"How'd you know where to find him?"

"Preston . . . Mr. Barrons . . . gave me his schedule."

Masoski arched an eyebrow and looked from Jennie to Preston and back.

Jennie didn't like the look. "If I were trying to get away, why would I stop on the fourth floor?"

"The guard said he saw the floor indicator moving. He wondered who was in the building and pushed the button to stop the elevator on the fourth floor. When the door opened, he apprehended you."

Jennie had to admit it didn't sound good. "Maybe he did push the button, and maybe that's the way it seemed to him, but I was looking for him. And I did tell him there was a body in Mr. Barrons' office." She spoke slowly, maintaining her calm with an effort.

Masoski held up a hand. "Let's leave it at that for now. What else did you see in that office?"

"Well, there was a gun."

"Where?"

"On the floor."

"Where on the floor?"

"I don't know exactly. I kicked it when I started to leave. That's when I became aware of it."

"Did you touch it?"

"No. Well, with my foot. I didn't pick it up, if that's what you mean."

"Had you ever seen the gun before?"

"I don't know. It looked like any gun to me. My father goes to an indoor shooting range sometimes. He has a pistol that looks kind of like that."

Masoski leaned forward. "Is it your father's gun?"

"I don't know how it could be."

"You didn't borrow the gun from your father?"

Before she could answer, Barrons said, "The gun probably belongs to me. I keep a pistol in my desk."

Masoski's face didn't change, nor his voice, but there was an alertness in his posture that hadn't been there before. "Any reason?" When no one spoke, he prompted, "For keeping a gun, I mean."

Barrons shook his head. "No reason. It's just something I do. My father kept one. So did my grandfather. Someday my son will probably keep a gun in his desk."

"Your son? Does he work at the bank, too?"

"Yes. For the summer. He'll go back to school in the fall. University of Mississippi."

Masoski said, "You have a license?"

"Of course."

"Is the gun usually loaded?"

"No. I keep cartridges in a separate drawer."

"Who knows about it?"

"I'm not sure. I don't flash it around. On the other hand, I've never attempted to hide it."

"So anyone who looked through your desk would see the gun?"

Preston nodded. "I suppose so."

"How many of your employees have access to your desk?"

Preston put his hand to his mouth. He looked stumped. "I don't know. I doubt many of them would go into my office and look through the drawers." He looked thoughtful. "The only one I can say for sure is Charlotte."

Masoski flipped back a couple of pages and looked at his notebook. "Charlotte? That's Mrs. Ellio, your secretary?"

"She prefers to be called administrative assistant." He shrugged, a manly gesture that left no doubt how he felt about that.

Masoski scribbled in his book before he went on. "What about the victim, Rob Payton? Did he have access to your desk?"

"He had no reason to go into my desk, but there was nothing to keep him out except respect for my privacy."

"Did he know about the gun?"

"I don't remember ever showing it to him. I never discussed it with anyone."

Masoski turned back to Jennie. "Did you know about the gun?"

"I've never been in that office before tonight. Never even been on this floor, in fact."

Preston said, "That's right."

One of the uniformed policemen stuck his head into the doorway. "You might want to look at this, Lieutenant."

Masoski said, "You three stay here," and he followed the cop out.

Jennie looked at Sunderson. "How much longer do you think this is going to take?"

He hunched his shoulders, then stood and stretched

his arms above his head. There were dark half-moons of perspiration on the underarms of his shirt. Even on him, the strain was beginning to show.

Jennie looked at her watch. 5:10. A little over three hours since she'd entered through the side door and climbed the stairs. Her head was pounding, and she felt as if she'd been dragged through an undersized knothole. She asked Barrons, "Is there any Advil around?"

"I believe Charlotte keeps some in her desk."

Jennie headed for the door.

Sunderson said, "The lieutenant said to stay here."

"I'm not going far."

Masoski trotted over as soon as she left the conference room. "Thought I told you to stay put."

"My head's killing me. I'm not much use to you if I can't think straight. Mr. Barrons said Mrs. Ellio might have some Advil in her desk. Besides, I have to use the bathroom."

Even with her head threatening to split and spill out thumbtacks, Jennie managed to take in the activity boiling around her. Most of it was concentrated in Preston's office. A metal gurney stood just outside the door. A black plastic bag with a zipper down the middle lay on top of it. Rob Payton. Jennie looked away. Inside the office, an irregular shape on the rug was marked out with tape. A woman in a white lab coat was crawling around on the floor.

Masoski took Jennie's arm and directed her away.

She asked, "Okay if I try to find something for my head in Mrs. Ellio's desk?"

He went with Jennie into the office next to Barrons' and watched while she opened the center drawer. "Didn't you look in her desk earlier?"

"I wasn't looking for Advil then, so I wouldn't have noticed if she had any." She closed the drawer and opened the top left one. A container of extra-strength Tylenol. Close enough. She looked at Masoski.

"Be my guest," he said. He pointed to the water cooler near the elevator. "Go ahead. I think the restrooms are over there, too. When you're finished, go back to the conference room and wait."

"Thanks."

Wait. That's what Masoski had said, and that's what Jennie, Sunderson, and Preston did, until dawn began to tint the conference room windows.

Preston moved to the other end of the room and pulled out his cell phone. He turned his back and spoke softly.

Jennie couldn't pick up every word, but it was clear he was talking to Leda. It sounded as if she didn't know where he was. How could she be unaware? They were married, presumably slept in the same bed. Surely she'd know if her husband got a phone call and left the house in the middle of the night. Didn't she ask where he was going?

Preston abandoned his soft tones. "I don't care about that! Wake him up and tell him to get his sorry butt in here!" With that, he snapped the phone shut and rejoined Jennie and Sunderson. "Web should be here soon," he said, though neither of them had asked for an explanation.

Chapter Six

Leda arrived a little after 6:00 A.M. with Web in tow.

Preston stood when he saw his wife and son get off the elevator but did not speak until they had crossed the threshold into the conference room. Then he gave Leda a perfunctory nod and focused on Web. "What time did you get in last night?" He barked the question with no preliminary greeting. There was no "Good morning, son," no touch of arm or shoulder, nothing to indicate a history, affectionate or otherwise, between the two.

Webster Barrons was twenty years old, but wide-set eyes the color of a summer sky made him seem younger. This morning those blue eyes were bloodshot and rimmed in red.

To Jennie, it looked as if the Barrons family heir had had a rough night and might be in for an even rougher morning.

The boy had inherited his mother's short, stocky build and, standing toe to toe, was looking at his father's chin—or would have been had he not been staring at the floor. "Pretty late, I guess."

"How many times have I told you to look me in the eye when you speak to me?" The veins in Preston's temples looked ready to pop.

Web took a seat and swiveled the chair to gaze out the window.

Preston walked around the table to confront him. "Where were you?"

The kid shrugged. "Around."

Leda bounced across the room and placed herself between father and son, facing the father. "This isn't easy for him."

Preston, Leda, and Web seemed unaware of anyone else.

Jennie wished she could disappear. She glanced toward the other non-family member in the room, Hamilton Sunderson. He had positioned himself in the doorway, so that his body screened the Barronses from anyone in the area outside the conference room. He watched the gathering storm through slitted eyes.

Preston spoke over Leda's shoulder. "Who were you with?"

Web still did not look at his father but remained slouched with his chin resting on his chest. "Nobody special. Different people, different places."

" 'Places'? You mean *bars*?"

Leda tried again. "Can we discuss this later?"

Sunderson cleared his throat and, when he had the attention of Preston, cut his eyes toward the area just beyond the open door, where Masoski stood talking to the security guard.

Preston Barrons glanced toward Masoski, then looked at the lawyer. He scowled at his son and said in a low voice, "You've got some explaining to do."

Web slouched lower in the chair.

The five of them—Jennie, the attorney, and the three Barronses—sat without speaking until the morning sun glinted on the windows.

In contrast, the area outside the conference room hummed. Lieutenant Masoski had apparently designated a desk near the center of the space as his operations center. A growing number of people, some in uniforms, some in street clothes, ebbed and flowed around this hub, creating an illusion of paths radiating outward to the elevator, the other desks, and the office where Jennie had discovered the body of Rob Payton.

The elevator *dinged.* Jennie glanced toward the sound, saw the doors part and a fifty-something woman step out. She heard Preston mutter, "There's Charlotte," and had to think a minute to realize he must mean Charlotte Ellio, his administrative assistant. She noted Preston checking his watch, and she glanced at hers. *A few minutes after eight. Is she always the first one in?* Jennie remembered that Ellio's office was one of those Preston had marked on the diagram of the sixth floor, one that she'd been asked to check out. Did that mean he thought Ellio might have made the funds transfer? How could she benefit from that? Or from the murder of Rob Payton?

Ellio stopped, looked around before she zeroed in on the group in the conference room, and headed toward them. Jennie studied her and thought she looked every inch an administrative assistant to the owner of a bank: just a tad overweight, dressed in a charcoal-gray jacket with lighter gray slacks and a pale-yellow blouse. Her short auburn hair was stylishly cut and waved back from her face.

A uniformed policeman intercepted her and motioned to a chair near the desk in the center of the room. Masoski was seated there, with the small spiral notebook cupped in one hand.

Ellio's expression and manner were composed when she sat down, her head tilted toward Masoski, her hands folded in her lap, legs demurely crossed at the ankle.

Jennie couldn't hear what was being said, but she could pinpoint the exact moment Ellio learned about Rob's death. The secretary reared back in the chair and put her hands in front of her mouth. Her purse fell off her lap and spilled keys and a lipstick onto the floor. Masoski chewed on his lower lip and watched as she stooped to pick them up, but he didn't offer to help. When she straightened up, he began speaking. After a few minutes, Ellio rose from the chair and went to the office next to Preston's.

Masoski didn't accompany her, but he didn't take his eyes off her until she returned to her position on the other side of the desk.

She was carrying a blue folder, which she handed to him.

Masoski opened the folder and studied it. He closed it, then said something to Ellio.

She nodded, spoke a few words, apparently in answer to Masoski's comment, then rose from her chair.

Masoski pointed to the group in the conference room. Ellio joined them.

Preston said, "Morning, Charlotte," but did not rise. "What's that you gave to the lieutenant?"

"Rob's personnel file."

Preston turned to Sunderson. "Do they have a right to see our files? Don't they need a subpoena or something?"

Sunderson said, "Let's not antagonize them." After a minute he asked, "Is there some reason you don't want them to see the files?"

The two men exchanged indecipherable glances.

Preston said, "No."

Ellio sat down across from Jennie.

Up close, Jennie noticed a quarter inch of white outlining the auburn in Ellio's hairline.

Quiet settled over the room until Leda remembered her manners. "Charlotte, Jennie, have you two met?"

"No." Both spoke at once and reached across the table to shake hands.

By 8:25 other employees began to arrive. All were met by a policeman when they got off the elevator. All were escorted to various desks, where, after a few words from the cop, they seated themselves. Jennie noted that the desks chosen were spaced far enough apart to make private conversation impossible. Any comments to a fellow employee would have to be loud enough to be heard by at least one of the law enforcement people. No one seemed eager to do this. They waited, docile as sheep, until, one by one, they were ushered to the chair opposite Masoski. Some, obviously nervous, made constant adjustments to their clothing or hair. Some were so elaborately casual, they seemed more nervous than their fidgeting co-workers. All, after their interview with Masoski, came to the conference room.

By 8:45 the twelve chairs around the massive teak table

were filled and three more had been carried in. There was much clearing of throats, many uneasy glances, but conversation was sparse.

Preston looked around; he seemed to be counting heads.

The elevator *dinged* again. All heads swiveled to watch the doors open. A tall man with a shock of thick, straw-colored hair stepped out. Masoski personally led him to the chair all had occupied before being granted access to the conference room.

"Ah, Karl. Everyone's here now." Charlotte Ellio's soft voice seemed to reverberate in the heavy silence.

Karl Erickson. Rob Payton's assistant. Jennie thought he seemed a little embarrassed when he looked over Masoski's shoulder toward the gathering in the conference room. His gaze lingered on Preston, who was looking at his watch. Again, Jennie checked hers. *About a minute before nine. Half an hour later than everyone else. And the boss is looking on.*

After his session with Masoski, Erickson joined the gathering. Except for Web, he was the youngest person there, appearing to be in his early twenties. He stood awkwardly in the doorway for a moment before he went to the end of the room and leaned against a wall.

One of the cops poked his head through the door and said, "Few minutes more and the lieutenant says you can get on with your jobs." He looked at Preston. "Come with me, please, sir."

Preston followed him.

Sunderson tagged along.

They were back in a couple of minutes. Preston said to

the group, "I've just spoken with Margaret on the phone."

It took Jennie a few seconds to process that he meant Rob Payton's wife.

Charlotte Ellio asked, "How is she?"

Preston shook his head. "Not good." His eyes sought Leda's. "I told her we'd come over. Lieutenant Masoski said it'd be okay."

Jennie said, "Any idea how much longer I have to stay?"

"The lieutenant said we can go about our business in a few minutes. He'll be in touch if he needs us. I assume he meant you, too."

Leda looked at Preston. "Maybe Web should drive her home."

Jennie said. "I have my car."

Preston looked toward the window. "Where did you leave it?"

"Out front."

Someone from the far end of the room said, "Probably been towed by now."

"That settles it. Web will drive you home." Leda was her usual assertive self again.

"But my car—"

Sunderson stepped forward. He looked first at Leda and Preston. "You two go on over to the Paytons. I'll take care of things here." He turned to Jennie. "You shouldn't be driving anyway. You've been up all night." He looked at Web. "Your mother's right. You take Mrs. Connors home." He looked back at Jennie. "I'll find out about your car."

"What about him?" Web inclined his head toward Masoski.

"I'll talk to him," Sunderson said, and he went to speak to the lieutenant.

"It's okay," he said when he returned. He looked toward Web. "He wants a statement from you, but it can wait."

Leda asked, "Why? What does he think Web knows about this?"

"He's taking statements from everyone who works on the sixth floor. Probably some others, too . . . anyone who had regular contact with Rob." His tone was conciliatory, as though soothing an anxious child.

Before Jennie and Web left, Sunderson conferred with Masoski again, then had Ellio make a photocopy of Jennie's driver's license. "Leave the key with me, and I'll arrange to have your car brought to you."

She fished her keys out of the backpack, removed one, and handed it to Sunderson.

Once Jennie settled into the BMW's plush leather seats, she had to fight to stay awake. She wasn't used to pulling all-nighters, and now that she was removed from the scene of the excitement, her lack of sleep was catching up with her. All she wanted to do was put her head back and escape the horror of the past few hours.

Web, on the other hand, seemed compelled to talk. "Of all people for this to happen to, why did it have to be Rob?" He stared over the steering wheel, shaking his head, then went on. "He was one of the nicest guys I know. Always ready to cut me a little slack. Everybody else was just waiting for me to fall on my can."

Jennie mumbled through her fog, "I doubt that's true."

"Believe me, it is. There's nothing more fun than seeing the boss's son make a fool of himself. Anybody else is five minutes late, it's no big deal. I'm five seconds late, and everybody looks at the clock and smirks. Worse yet, they say, 'Morning, Web' loudly enough to make sure Dad hears."

The tension in Web's voice caught Jennie's attention. "Rob never did that?"

"No, just the opposite—he helped me cover up a couple of mistakes so Dad wouldn't find out."

She was wide-awake now. "What kind of mistakes?" She studied Web's profile while she waited for an answer.

His jaw was clenched, with a hint of muscles struggling for control. He removed one hand from the steering wheel and waggled it. "Little things." He grew quiet, then finally said, "Still, if the old man ever found out, he'd kill us both." The minute the words were out, their significance seemed to hit Web. He looked at Jennie, then quickly back at the road. "I didn't mean . . ." He puffed his cheeks and blew out the air.

"Don't worry, I didn't take it literally." When the quiet became uncomfortable, Jennie added, "Whether you realize it or not, your father loves you. He just—"

Web finished for her, "Wants to make a man of me."

"That's not what I was going to say." It wasn't, but it was close to what she was thinking.

"But it's true. Nothing I do pleases him."

"He just expects a lot. Parents do that. Doesn't mean they aren't proud of you. I haven't been around your father much, but I can tell you, there's nobody prouder of their son than your mother is of you."

"Yeah, I know. And, believe me, it's a heavy burden.

Dad's always trying to make a man out of me, and she's always making excuses. Then he gets mad because I don't speak for myself. Doesn't seem to realize it's hard to get a word in before Mom does." Web glanced over at Jennie and grinned. "Two go-get-'em parents and one screwup son."

"Hang in there. It'll get better." Even to Jennie, it sounded lame.

Web didn't comment.

She moved on to the thing that had been bothering her all morning. "Your mother didn't seem to know that your father had left the house."

Still no comment.

Jennie persisted. "She must be a sound sleeper. I mean, her husband gets a phone call in the middle of the night and leaves, and she doesn't even know he's gone?" She knew she was being heavy-handed, even nosy, but figured she had a right to an explanation.

Web finally spoke. "Dad has insomnia. When he can't sleep, he goes to the library and reads." He shrugged. "Who knows? Maybe the guard called his cell. Mom wouldn't hear that."

"That makes sense." *And maybe he wasn't even home.* She looked over at Web. "You must be as tired as I am. You been up all night, too?"

"Yeah. And the old man's gonna make me pay for it."

Jennie probed a little deeper. "Have a good time with your friends?"

"Actually, I was alone. Barhoppin'."

"You old enough to drink legally?"

He rubbed his thumb over his fingers. "There's ways around that."

And I bet you know 'em all. "Is it worth it? I mean, barhopping by yourself doesn't sound like much fun."

He shrugged. "I was hoping I'd run into somebody."

"You never did? All night long?"

"Nope."

So, nobody in the family can vouch for anybody else. Three lone rangers.

Chapter Seven

Jennie almost put her foot through the floorboard when Web stopped the BMW a scant six inches short of her garage door.

"Thanks," she said, and she stepped from the car. She paused to run her fingertips over the BMW's gleaming silver rooftop, leaned down, and added, "After my Bug, this car's a treat."

"Yeah, it's nice. Being Preston Barrons' kid isn't all bad." He patted the dash. "Guess I shouldn't complain."

Jennie heard the wistful sadness behind his words and wished she knew how to bridge the gap between father and son. "You wouldn't be human if you didn't. Maybe you need to cut your parents a little slack, though."

He shrugged, backed out, and peeled away.

Jennie watched the M5 roar down the street and careen around the corner. *Thank God there aren't any kids around.*

At 10:00 A.M. it was already sweltering, and most of

the neighborhood kids were either at the pool or tucked away somewhere air-conditioned. The streets of the neat suburban neighborhood were quiet. Web was a threat to no one but himself.

Jennie told herself she had problems of her own—the Barronses would have to take care of themselves—and headed for the shower.

Seconds later, needles of warm water massaged her shoulders and back. She soaped her skin with the lavender-scented bar of soap and breathed its calming essence in the steam rising around her. *Heavenly.*

After the luxury of a long shower with no interrupting "Mom!"'s or even a ringing telephone, Jennie was ready for an even greater luxury—rest. She called Riverview, told them she wouldn't be in until afternoon, then pulled the sheet up under her chin and waited for sleep to come. It didn't. Part by part, starting with her toes, she willed her body to relax. It wouldn't. Her senses tingled, recalling recent stimuli. Her calf muscles relived the ascent of six flights of stairs, her stomach the swaying of a descending elevator, and, most of all, her fingertips recoiled from the stiff, non-human feel of Rob Payton's wrist. She closed her eyes and tried to visualize a meadow filled with daisies. No good. She saw instead the photograph of Rob and his wife on the golf cart. *Music.* She got up, selected a Mozart concerto, and placed the portable CD player on the pillow next to her. Even that didn't help.

Twenty minutes later, she was on the phone, calling a cab. Next, she called Hamilton Sunderson and asked him to have her car delivered to Riverview Manor when he freed it from the parking authority.

He tried to discourage her. "You've been up all night. Shouldn't you get some sleep?"

"I tried that. It didn't work."

"But—"

"I can't stay here by myself."

"You're afraid?"

"That's not it. I need to be around people."

There was a long pause, followed by a slowly expelled breath. "Be careful what you say. We have a sensitive situation to deal with."

"Don't worry. I'm going in to keep from thinking about what happened. I don't plan to even mention last night."

At the last second, when she saw the cab pull into the driveway, Jennie grabbed the backpack. *Maybe I'll have a chance to look through this stuff when everyone's at lunch. Sooner or later Masoski's going to ask if I found anything, and I'll have to give it to him.* She wondered how much trouble she'd be in for not leaving the bag with him in the first place. *Well, he didn't ask for it.*

"Here. This is perfect," Jennie told the driver when he pulled up behind Riverview Manor.

The door from the parking lot led directly into an open lounge area with a reception desk tucked in one corner. She glanced at the clock above the desk. Almost 11:00. No one noticed Jennie's arrival. Maybe she could keep her promise to Sunderson and avoid talking about her discovery. She'd heard a news report of the murder on the cab radio, but there'd been no mention of her name.

The lounge was furnished with couches, chairs, and small tables arranged in conversation groupings. The faint scent of a lemon air freshener hung in the air. A huge bird-cage occupied most of one wall. This morning the couches and chairs were empty. A dozen residents clustered near the birdcage, staring at an egg the size of her smallest fingernail.

"He's about to break through."

"Shh! You'll scare the mother, and she might hurt him." Tess Zumwalt spoke in a soft peep. It sounded like the voice of someone who might know how a mother bird would feel.

Jennie crowded closer and looked over the shoulder of a woman in a wheelchair.

Doreen Tull turned to smile at her.

"Hi," Jennie said. "Big day's finally here, huh?"

"Yes. It looks like the little ones are ready to hatch."

A deep, theatrical voice from behind the group boomed, "Ah, Jennifer, you're here. Didn't know if we'd see you today."

Jennie turned to greet Nathaniel Pynchon. "Where else would I be?"

"I thought her ladyship might have other plans for you." The former actor inclined his head toward the corridor leading to the Executive Director's office.

Georgia Peterson, a ninety-year-old of deceptively fragile appearance, joined them. "Why would Leda have plans for Jennie today?"

Nate sighed impressively. "I shouldn't be surprised that no one except me listens to the news."

Now that he had everyone's attention, Nate affected indifference.

Georgie flounced over, hands on hips and glared up at him. "Well, are you going to tell us or not?"

"Tell you what?"

Georgie turned away. "Forget it. We'll read about it in the newspaper. Then, at least, we'll know we have it right."

Threatened with losing his audience, Nate spoke quickly. "There was a murder at Preston Barrons' bank last night."

The birdcage was forgotten, and residents closed in around Nate.

Jennie took advantage of the confusion to sneak away to the corner of the Activities Room that served as her office. She spread the contents of the backpack on her desk and sorted them into three piles: one for Rob Payton's office, one for Karl Erickson's, and one for Charlotte Ellio's. She lay the envelope with the charred paper off to one side.

She looked at the three stacks and thought about the death and the funds transfer. *Were the two crimes related?* Instinct told her they must be. *Did his murder mean that Rob had made the transfer? Or did it clear him?* She pondered this. The contents of the envelope must point to a guilty secret. *Nobody burns innocent bits of paper.* If Rob had stolen the money and tried to frame Web Barrons for it, would Leda or Preston kill him? She had a hard time envisioning either of them resorting to anything that drastic. Still, you couldn't dismiss what a parent might do when their child is threatened. And both Preston and Leda were proud people. What about Web himself? Jennie had seen enough of him over her years at Riverview to know he wasn't long on self-control. And, as Tom had pointed out, the kid was neither a Boy Scout nor a genius.

And then there was the big question, the one that bothered Jennie most: had Leda and Preston been honest about their reason for sending her into the bank? Did they know what she would find? Preston had come to her defense with Masoski. He hadn't hesitated to admit he'd supplied her with the key. These ideas chased one another through her mind until the sound of approaching footsteps warned her she'd have to pursue them later.

Nate appeared first. "How come you were late this morning?" When Jennie didn't answer immediately, he persisted. "You knew about the murder, didn't you?"

Georgie was next. "Is that true?"

Jennie knew she'd have to deal with the residents' reactions to the missing money and the murder sooner or later—and it looked like sooner. "Yes, I did."

People kept appearing until the majority of residents of the North Wing, the area of the retirement facility where the healthiest, most mobile residents lived, had gathered in the Activities Room. All turned expectant faces toward Jennie.

A voice from the corner asked, "Did Leda tell you about it?"

"Not exactly."

Something in her tone must have tipped them off. They crowded closer. Everyone fired questions at the same time, until the voices blended, sounding like a louder version of the chirping in the birdcage.

Jennie's cell phone rang. She made the familiar *T* sign with her hands before she grabbed the phone. "Hello."

"Mrs. Connors? This is Lieutenant Masoski."

"Yes, Lieutenant." She spoke loudly enough for the residents to hear, and she put a finger to her lips, wishing they'd all tiptoe away. They became mute, but no one left.

"I wasn't finished with you."

"Mr. Sunderson told me you said I could go."

"Never mind that. Did you find anything when you searched the offices?"

She glanced at the papers spread over the desk, focusing on the envelope. "Actually, I think I might have."

"Oh?"

"There were scraps of burned paper in the bottom of Rob Payton's trash can."

"Did you remove them?"

She wondered what Hamilton Sunderson would advise her to do. *The heck with him. I'm going to just tell the truth and walk away.* She took a deep breath. "Yes. I put them into an envelope."

"Where's the envelope now?"

"Here, with me, at Riverview."

"Anything else?"

"I put some papers I found in wastebaskets into my backpack."

"What kind of papers?"

"I don't know. I was going through the trash cans when I heard something. I went to check, and that's when I found the body."

She looked up to see the residents exchanging meaningful looks.

Masoski's voice demanded her full attention. "Did you remove anything else from the bank?"

"No."

"Why didn't you give me those papers this morning?"

"I didn't think about it. You were busy. Sunderson said I could go. I just grabbed my backpack and left."

"Where is the backpack now?"

"It's here."

"I'll pick it up in twenty minutes."

"Fine."

"I expect everything you left the building with to be in that backpack."

"It will be." She looked at the residents standing on the other side of her desk. They looked planted, with roots reaching to the center of the earth. No hope of their leaving until they had an explanation. "You guys have a right to know about this. I'm not sure if it will affect you, but it might. So . . ."

She gave them a quick rundown of the past twenty-four hours, ending with: "Lieutenant Masoski will be here in about fifteen minutes to pick this up." She waved toward the backpack. Nobody moved. She held out her arm with the watch on it. "It's lunchtime. Why don't you all go to the dining room? I'll wait here for Masoski. If you want to know more, come back after lunch, and I'll fill you in as much as I can."

There were murmurs of agreement, and most of them left.

Jennie was surprised that the one person who remained was Tess Zumwalt, possibly Riverview's most mild-mannered resident.

Tess stood there, looking like the quintessential grandmother: tight gray curls, brown eyes that gave no hint of her thoughts, loose-fitting tan trousers, a pink cardigan with a white linen handkerchief escaping its pocket. She said, "Sounds like a setup to me." She cocked her head to one side. "Question is, who's setting up whom?"

Jennie shrugged. "I think my best bet is to let the police handle it. I'm pretty sure Masoski knows I'm telling the truth."

Tess tilted her head the other way and continued to stare at Jennie.

Jennie stared back. "You have a better idea?" This was not like Tess. Her usual style was to blend in, make no waves. Then the light went on. "You used to work for the FBI, didn't you?"

Tess nodded. "As a graphologist."

"Handwriting analyst, right?"

"Yes." Tess busied herself gathering the papers. "I heard you promise not to remove any of these." She stopped to smile slyly at Jennie. "Nobody said we can't copy them."

Jennie glanced at her watch. "We've got ten minutes."

Tess helped her replace the papers in the backpack. They headed for the copier in the conference room. When they went in, Jennie started to close the door behind them.

Tess stopped her. "A closed door is an invitation to see what's behind it."

"In other words, we don't want anyone to know what we're doing."

Tess didn't comment on that. She handed a sheaf of papers to Jennie; they were the ones she'd removed from Payton's office. "You start copying. I'll see if I can learn anything from this." She held up the envelope with the charred fragments in it.

By the time Jennie was finished with the first batch, Tess had given up on the burned paper. "Nothing left to see," she said, "but the fact somebody burned them tells us something."

"The challenge is to find out what," Jennie said.

Tess said, "You're learning," and she handed over three pieces of paper with a roadmap-like network of creases. They were from Karl Erickson's office, the ones that had been wadded up. Jennie copied them. Tess handed over more. They worked quickly, an efficient team. While Jennie was copying the last of the papers, Tess looked over the newspapers from Charlotte Ellio's desk. "Don't bother with these," she said. "The marked items are real estate ads. All for small apartment buildings."

"What about locations?" Jennie asked. "Should we write those down?"

"No time. Just remember she's looking at income-producing properties." As she spoke, Tess opened the drawer on a nearby console, selected a manila folder, and put the copies in. Then she replaced the original papers in the backpack. When they were all in, she reached in and stirred them up a little. "For that tousled, natural appearance." She flashed a lopsided grin, suggestive of a five-year-old sneaking a cookie, and handed the backpack to Jennie. Then she slipped the manila folder under a stack of books on the console. "I'll pick this up later and take it to my room." She stepped back to survey the arrangement, made a minute adjustment, pushing the folder's edge farther under the books, and gave a thumbs-up sign to Jennie. "Okay, lunchtime for me."

"And I'll go wait for Masoski."

"Stop in the dining hall. Chat a minute. That way, if he's already here and wants to know where you were, you have a good answer."

"And I won't have to lie."

Tess's roguish smile was back. She waved a finger at

Jennie. "Never lie," she said. "Evade all you can, but never, ever lie to the authorities."

Jennie threw back her head and laughed. "You're full of surprises."

"Most people are. Remember that."

Chapter Eight

Masoski was pacing the length of the Activities Room when Jennie got there.

Before she'd crossed the threshold, he snapped at her. "Where were you?"

Thank you, Tess. Jennie suppressed a smile. "In the dining hall." She went straight to her desk and swung the backpack up onto its surface. "Here's what you're looking for."

"Why'd you take it with you?"

"I didn't think you'd want me to leave it lying around."

He grunted and opened the pack. "Everything here?"

"Yes."

"You didn't remove anything?"

She remembered Tess's advice. "Yes, but it's all there now. I put everything back."

"Why'd you remove it in the first place?" He glared from under bushy eyebrows that formed an almost solid line when he frowned.

65

"To look at. I put it back after you called." So far, so good. Everything she'd said was true.

Masoski held the pack at arm's length. "Not what I was expecting when you said backpack." He plopped into a nearby chair.

The item in question was constructed along the lines of a traditional backpack but was about half the size and made of a quilted paisley fabric in shades of burgundy and gold. There were numerous pockets, zipper closures, and wide straps that slipped over the shoulders.

Jennie ran her fingertips along one strap. "My grand-mother's a quilter. She made this for me." She looked at him. "I'll get it back, won't I?"

"When I'm finished with it." He leaned forward and rested his hands on his knees, with the backpack dangling from his thumbs. "Tell me again exactly what time you entered the bank premises."

"We went over all that last night. At least a hundred times. It was just a little after two."

"You said in your statement it was two-oh-eight."

"Well, isn't that—"

"Two-oh-eight is a very precise time."

"I remember checking my watch when I started up the stairs. I don't remember the exact time anymore, but if I said two-oh-eight last night, that's when it was." She heard the edge in her voice and took a slow, deep breath. *He's just doing his job.* She met his gaze and forced a smile, determined not to antagonize him more than she already had.

He asked, "Where were you at midnight?"

"Home, watching a late movie."

"Alone?"

She refrained from reminding him that she'd already given him the information and answered with a simple, "Yes."

"What was the movie?"

"I'm not sure. PBS had an all-Bogart night. I watched *Key Largo*, then a couple more until it was time to leave. I guess I dozed off and on."

Masoski looked as if he wanted to know more.

She tried to remember the sequence of the movies. "Around midnight I think it was probably *African Queen*. Why?"

"Never mind." He chewed his lip, stared, and seemed to be looking through, not at, her. It was clear he didn't intend to answer the question. He rose from the chair and was in the hall before Jennie remembered that her wallet was in the backpack. She ran after him. "Hey, wait. My personal stuff's in there, too. I need it."

"What kind of stuff?"

"My driver's license, for one thing."

He held out the pack and watched Jennie remove her wallet. Then, without comment, he took the wallet from her and flipped through its contents before he tossed it back.

Jennie didn't know why, but she felt compelled to explain. "I used the pack as a purse last night."

Masoski hadn't been gone long when residents started drifting back. All had questions to ask. All were unwilling to wait their turn. Multiple voices merged into one, a static-filled babel, impossible to understand, even more impossible to answer.

Nate, never happy unless he was center stage, took

charge. He stood beside Jennie and held up both hands. "Let's all be quiet and let Jennie tell us what happened." She started to protest. "I don't think—"

Nate wouldn't let her finish. "That murder at the bank might affect our trust money. We have a right to know what's going on." His British roots were evident in every precisely enunciated syllable, adding authority to his words.

Georgie spoke up. "I heard the funds raised at the Gala were stolen."

An oppressive quiet settled over the room. Riverview Manor, a private retirement community and nursing facility, was an expensive place to live. Most of the residents were well able to afford the luxury and choice offered by private care, but some needed a little help from time to time. A special account was maintained to supplement monthly fees or to help out with unforeseen expenses. Income from the Cardamon Trust formed the backbone of the Special Account. The trust had been set up by a prominent Memphis family with ties to Riverview. Leda and Preston Barrons, along with Harold Cardamon, the only member of the family still living, and Attorney Hamilton Sunderson, controlled the purse strings. According to the terms of the trust, income was to be used "to make the lives of Riverview Manor's citizens more pleasant."

Jennie's position as Activities Director was funded by income from the trust. Leda had explained to Jennie that the language chosen was deliberately broad. It had been the intent of the Cardamon family that, except in extreme cases, persons who came to Riverview in affluent times were not to be put out because of the vagaries of personal fortune. Since the principal was large and wisely invested, money was always available to help residents experiencing financial difficulties. In addition, an annual fund-raising event supplemented the income generated by the trust. This year's Gala had yielded $68,750, not a huge sum compared to the billions and trillions mentioned routinely in the news, but it was a nice cushion, a cherry atop the security sundae provided by the trust.

In the two years Jennie had worked as Activities Director of Riverview, she'd become champion and confidante of most of the residents. As she looked out at the faces before her, she felt confident she fulfilled the criteria of "making their lives more pleasant" and wondered what the Cardamon family would think of Leda and Preston's withholding her salary unless she helped clear their son.

The faces displayed a variety of emotions. Some appeared angry, some frightened. All looked betrayed. She suspected it was not the money as much as the knowledge that something was threatening their security.

Georgie served as resident representative on Riverview's Board of Directors. She asked, "Is it true? Is the money gone?"

Jennie said, "No. It's not gone."

"Then what happened? Is the story I heard false?"

"It's more complex than that."

Nate repeated his earlier statement. "We have a right to know what's going on."

A different voice inserted itself into the debate. "Going on about what?"

Jennie looked past the residents to see Leda and Preston

Barrons standing in the doorway. It was Leda who had spoken.

The residents all shifted to face the Executive Director and her husband.

Jennie said, "They heard news reports about the murder. They've also heard a rumor that the money from the Gala was stolen."

Both Barronses stared at her with stony faces.

Jennie lifted her chin and went on. "They want to know what happened. I think they have that right. You can explain it better than I can."

After a quick glance at his wife, Preston strode to the front of the room and stood by Jennie. "This is going to take a few minutes. Perhaps you'd all like to sit down."

The Activities Room was furnished with an assortment of lightweight furniture that could be arranged in multiple configurations. As Preston finished speaking, Jennie and some of the residents began moving chairs into rows. Preston and Leda dragged a table to the front of the room and placed two chairs facing outward.

Jennie was surprised when Leda took a seat and smiled up at her husband. Riverview Manor was Leda's baby, and, under normal circumstances, any statements concerning that baby came from her.

Preston's expression must have conveyed the same wonder, because Leda said, "The events all concerned your bank. You're in a better position than I am to answer questions."

He bowed, a caricature of a southern gentleman deferring to his lady.

His audience was attentive. If the proverbial pin had dropped, it would have resounded like a bowling ball.

Preston began with the disappearance of the money from Riverview's Special Account, admitted that it had shown up in their son, Web's, personal account, and ended with the discovery by Jennie of Rob Payton's body. When he was finished, he looked at Jennie. "Is there anything you want to add?"

"No." She was, in fact, impressed by the straightforward manner in which Preston had conveyed the information. As far as she could discern, there had been no attempt at spin.

Preston's gaze swept the faces of the residents. "Any questions?"

Nate asked, "Where's the money now?"

Leda stood up beside her husband. "It's been transferred back to Riverview's Special Account." She bit her lip and added, "I hope all of you realize that none of this is the doing of my son. Someone is trying to frame Web." She held her head higher. "They will not get away with it. They will be found out and punished. Rest assured of that." The final statement came through clenched teeth.

Nate persisted, "If one of us needs money, will it be available?"

Jennie watched Preston and Leda exchange glances.

Preston finally spoke. "The trust account is frozen until we find out who made the unauthorized transfer."

Leda said, "You must understand, this step was taken to protect the trust. It's in your best interests."

Nate asked, "In the meantime, what if one of us needs money?"

Leda said, "If that happens, come to me. I'll find a way to deal with it."

Preston looked meaningfully at his watch, grabbed his

wife's arm, and steered her to the door without making eye contact with anyone in the room.

There was silence for a few seconds, then the group separated into small cliques, which, one by one, flowed out into the hall. Jennie watched them go, observed heads bent close in whispering conversation, and pondered what her next move should be. Should there be a next move? Was there really any reason for her to be personally involved? Surely the combined expertise of Lieutenant Masoski and the bank's IT guru would discover who had transferred the money and the trust funds would be freed. It was just a question of time.

She reached for a notepad and started a list of bills to be paid.

Her phone rang. "Hello."

"In all the excitement, I didn't get a chance to ask if you were successful." Obviously Preston didn't think it necessary to identify himself.

"You mean, did I find anything to tell us who made the transfer?"

"Yes."

"I don't know. I started out looking at papers on desks, but I realized you had probably already checked that, so I concentrated on wastebaskets. Since I was in a hurry, I put everything into my backpack to take home and read later."

"And?"

Jennie continued, "Lieutenant Masoski came by just before you got here and took the backpack with him."

"It's gone?"

"Yes."

"Did you have time to examine what you had?"

"No." Not a lie. Jennie still hadn't had time to look over the copies she'd made—and, for some reason, she decided not to tell Preston about them. She said, "The only things I saw that seemed suspicious were some burned scraps in the bottom of Rob Payton's wastebasket. They were pretty much destroyed. No writing remained." She waited, curious what he would say about that.

"Well, that's that. If you don't have them, you don't have them."

The words didn't convey any reaction to the destroyed papers. She wished she could see his face.

"Let us know if you need anything." He sounded ready to say good-bye.

Jennie glanced down at the list she was working on. "What about my salary? It may take a while to clear this up. I can't—"

"Don't worry. We'll see that you're taken care of." With that, he hung up.

Taken care of. Sounds like something you'd call a plumber for.

She heard a throat being cleared and looked up.

Tess came in and sat down. "What's this about your salary?"

After Jennie gave her a rundown on the conversation with Preston, Tess said, "In other words, the Barronses have made you dependent on their good will."

"Looks that way."

"Did you tell him about the copies?"

Jennie grinned. "He didn't ask."

Tess grinned back and winked. "You're learning."

"Have you had a chance to look at any of the handwriting samples?"

"Just a glance. Not enough to form any clear opinions."

Jennie hesitated, then asked, "What'd you think of Leda's little speech?"

"You mean about none of this being Web's doing?"

"Yes."

Tess shrugged. "Hard to say. Knowing how Leda dotes on that boy, it's what I'd expect. She'd believe anything he said. On the other hand . . . maybe she doesn't believe him. A mother will defend her young—innocent or guilty—in fact, she'll fight harder if she knows he's guilty."

"Since you're a graphologist . . ." Jennie paused and let Tess fill in the rest. "Maybe we should we get samples of writing from Leda and Preston. Web, too. Especially Web."

"Excellent idea. You want to take on that little project?" Tess replied.

Chapter Nine

Jennie went through her files and selected a long hand-written memo from Leda.

She hummed, feeling almost hopeful as she walked along the corridor to Tess's room. At the very least, this should be interesting. Jennie didn't have a lot of contact with Tess except at the tea ladies' monthly gathering. This group of half a dozen residents assembled for a formal high tea one Saturday afternoon a month. Georgie Peterson was the most outspoken and gregarious of the group, though Doreen Tull was their unofficial leader. Dependent on a wheelchair for mobility, Doreen, a talented artist, kept Georgie in line with a firm but subtle, hand. Tess was the quietest member of the group. She let the others do most of the talking, only occasionally adding a wry but always relevant comment.

As Jennie approached the lounge, raised voices rolled out to greet her. Jennie stopped to see what was up.

Nate, not surprisingly, was in the thick of it. " 'Confusion now hath made his masterpiece,' " rumbled from his throat in mellifluous tones.

Georgie's honeyed drawl glided back. "If anybody's confused, it's you. The trust is safe. You're just looking for something to complain about."

Nate abandoned Shakespeare. "That's easy for you to say. You don't have to worry about money. Your husband left you with a fat bank account."

Georgie bristled and stepped forward, fire in her eyes. Jennie glanced around. Other residents watched, grinning, apparently enjoying the excitement and looking forward to more. The only person present who could reasonably be expected to step in was Alice Telford. Jennie sighed. *Fat chance.* Alice was a childhood friend of Leda's and her assistant. No one was better at handling meticulous detail than Alice—and no one was worse at dealing with conflict. Jennie knew it was up to her to keep the spat from becoming a real brouhaha.

She took Nate's arm and said, "Georgie's right. The funds in the trust are safe. The freeze is temporary." In a lower tone, she added, "There's no reason to be nasty to Georgie. None of this is her fault."

Nate shrugged eloquently.

Georgie said to Jennie, "Don't worry. I don't expect an apology from him . . . unless it's a quote. He doesn't write his own lines." Sarcasm dripped from every syllable. In her own way, Georgie was as accomplished a performer as Nate.

Nate pivoted on his heel and stalked off toward his room. Even from the back, he projected wronged indignation.

Georgie kept her eyes on Jennie. "Is that right? Are the funds safe?" When Jennie didn't answer immediately, she said, "As Resident Advisor to the trust, I have a right to know."

"They're safe," Jennie assured her, reasonably sure she was speaking the truth.

Georgie looked skeptical but didn't press for more detail. She settled herself in a wing chair and directed her attention to the TV, where the residents' favorite soap opera was playing.

Jennie watched for a minute before she continued toward Tess's room. When she reached it, she took time to study the woman sitting by the window. There was a book in her lap and a knitting bag on the floor beside her chair. The seventy-four-year-old widow was about five-three, neither fat nor thin. Her hair was gray and formed a halo of permed curls around a sweet face. Glasses with thin steel rims slid halfway down an aquiline nose that looked as if it had been broken at least once. Jennie knew Tess had grown up with three older brothers. She wondered if the nose was a casualty of too exuberant roughhousing with her siblings. Or had her FBI career taken its toll? Looking at the grandmotherly figure, Jennie found either scenario hard to believe. Still, people were full of surprises. Who'd have expected Tess to anticipate Masoski's actions and to give such good advice about dealing with him? If Tess had been a man, Jennie might have asked about the nose. A man might pride himself on a history of violent confrontation. Some women might, too. Tess did not seem like one who would. She seldom spoke of her past, one of the few Riverview residents who did not. Most of them loved to reminisce.

Tess looked up. "Well, are you coming in?"

"Yes," Jennie said. "That is, if it's okay. I thought you forgot I was coming."

"Is that why you've been standing there so long?"

"I didn't think you knew I was here." Jennie realized it sounded as if she was snooping and added, "Not that I meant to spy on you. You seemed absorbed in your book. I didn't want to interrupt."

Tess held out her hand. "Let's see what you have."

Jennie gave her the page filled with Leda's handwritten instructions. "I found this in my file. Thought it would be a good starting place."

Tess scanned the pages of the memo quickly. Too quickly, it seemed to Jennie, to be making any kind of analysis.

When Tess looked up, she said, "No surprises here. An unusually well-organized script style."

Jennie sat in Tess's extra chair. "What, exactly, do you mean?"

Tess held the paper out and ran her index finger over a line of writing. "Look. The letters retain the same shape consistently. That indicates someone who knows her own mind."

"Sounds like our Leda. Anything else?"

Tess removed a six-inch plastic ruler from the drawer of a small chest between the two chairs. She lay the edge under a line of Leda's writing. "See how the letters sit on the baseline?"

"Yes."

"The mark of a realist, someone with good planning ability." She moved the ruler so its edge lined up vertically along a small *d*. "Almost straight up and down."

Jennie leaned closer. "Oh?"

"Sure indication of someone who has a reason for everything she does."

A male voice asked, "Who has?"

Both women looked up.

Nate came in without waiting for an invitation. He repeated, "Who has a reason for everything she does?"

Jennie wished she'd thought to close the door behind her when she'd come into the room. Open doors at Riverview proclaimed welcome. Anyone who wanted privacy or time alone closed the door, a signal that was universally respected. Well, almost universally. Even a closed door didn't always stop Nate. Despite his flaunting of rules, or maybe because of it, Nate was a favorite of Jennie's. This time, however, she preferred not to involve him. She glanced at Tess.

If Tess cared, she didn't show it. "We're analyzing someone's handwriting," she said, and she held the paper out.

Jennie noticed that her thumb covered Leda's name in the *From* line.

"Let me see," Nate said.

Tess smiled angelically and wrinkled her nose at him. "I doubt you'd be interested. This is just a silly little thing Jennie and I are whiling away the time with."

Nate looked doubtful, but he left without argument.

Jennie said, "I've never seen him give up so easily."

"The trick to winning battles is not getting into them."

"Wish you'd teach Georgie that."

"And miss all the fun?" Tess' smile was pure mischief.

Jennie pointed to the page of notes. "Tell me more."

"Okay. See how—"

Alice appeared in the doorway. "Jennie, you have a phone call."

"Can you take a message? Tell them I'll call back later?"

"I think you'd better take it now." Alice's voice held more conviction than usual.

Jennie tried to hide her annoyance and followed Alice into the hall. "Who is it?"

Alice darted a worried look Jennie's way and whispered, "Mrs. Payton."

"As in the wife of Rob Payton?"

Alice nodded.

Ohmigod! What do you say to a woman whose husband has just been murdered? Especially if you're the one who found the body?

Alice kept walking, leading Jennie toward Leda's office. "You'd better take it in here. This is the most private place."

Jennie picked up the phone. "Mrs. Payton? Jennifer Connors here. I am so sorry—"

"Yes, I know you're sorry. Everyone's sorry. But nobody's sorry enough to come out and say the name of the person we all know is guilty of this vicious crime." Even over the phone, the anger behind her words was unmistakable.

"I don't understand."

"Oh, I think you do. I think you know as well as I do who murdered my husband."

"I . . . uh . . ." Jennie heard herself stammering and stopped.

Margaret Payton said, "You found Rob. I want to know the details."

Jennie's mind raced. She tried to think how to respond.

Margaret went on. "Come to my house this afternoon. At least tell me what my husband's last moments on this earth were like." Her voice had gone from angry to pleading, climbing higher with each word. "Please." The last word was a sob.

Jennie knew she had to go.

Chapter Ten

Jennie kept to her own lane and didn't take advantage of the VW Bug's small size to maneuver in the rush-hour traffic. This afternoon, she welcomed each slowdown. Every red light postponed the moment when she'd have to face Rob Payton's widow.

She spotted the shopping center she'd been told to use as a landmark and turned into an upscale East Memphis neighborhood. Traffic, even at five-thirty in the afternoon, was sparse on the shady side streets. The few cars she encountered moved slowly. An elderly couple walked a dog. Kids were out on skateboards. A teenaged boy alternately pushed a lawnmower and tugged up his sagging cargo pants.

Jennie looked for 4843 and, when she saw it, pulled in behind a maroon SUV. She took a minute to study the brick ranch house before she faced the widow.

The Bermuda grass lawn resembled a miniature golf course. Boxwood hedges were manicured. Twin magnolias, with limbs trimmed high, framed the front door like oversized bouquets. On this first day of July, there were no blossoms left, but the broad leaves were as smooth and glistening as a satin gown. Walkway and wide steps were constructed of the same antique brick as the house. An iron gate with a *P* worked into its lacy pattern formed an outdoor vestibule between steps and entry, preventing visitors from getting too close without an invitation.

The door behind the gate opened, and a broad-shouldered woman stepped out. She was dressed as if for church, in a navy skirt and matching jacket with a lighter blue blouse and low-heeled pumps. Ginger-colored hair was tucked behind her ears with sections escaping in untidy clumps. Her fair skin was blotchy, her eyes underscored with dark circles. She offered her hand. "I'm Margaret Payton. We met last weekend at the Gala."

"Yes, I remember." Jennie grasped the outstretched hand and added, "I'm so sorry about your husband."

Margaret acknowledged the condolences with a nod and beckoned Jennie to follow. She led the way into a family room dominated by a stone fireplace. Shelves, filled with a multitude of trophies and a few books, lined two walls. Framed photographs rested atop an upright piano.

A phone rang in an adjoining room. A woman's voice answered. Words barely above a whisper drifted out to them. "She's not taking calls. Would you like to leave a message?"

When the murmuring voice stopped, Margaret went to the doorway. "Would you mind using the phone in the bedroom for a while?"

A woman, clutching a pad of paper and several pens, came into the room.

Margaret introduced them. "Jennie Connors, Beth Evanston. She's been fielding calls for me." Her voice caught in her throat. "I don't know what I'd do without her."

Beth nodded in Jennie's direction, gave Margaret a brief hug, then disappeared down the hall.

Margaret dropped heavily into an upholstered chair and waved to the love seat nearby. She chewed on her thumbnail and studied Jennie before she spoke. "The police said you saw someone leaving Preston's office but don't who it was."

"That's not quite accurate. I heard activity in his office, and a few minutes later I noticed that the elevator was going down. I figured someone had been in there and left. I went in to check, and that's when I . . ."

"That's when you found my husband?" Margaret's face and voice were stony.

"Yes. But I didn't see anyone else in Preston's office. I went in because of something I thought I'd heard. I didn't—"

"You're lying. I know you're lying!" Margaret's voice climbed, threatening to go out of control. "You saw Web Barrons, and you're covering up for him, like everyone else. Just like everyone's done his whole life. You—" She stopped, apparently distracted by something behind Jennie. A horrified expression descended over her features.

Jennie turned.

A beautiful waif, accompanied by two schnauzers, stood in the doorway. It was the young girl she'd seen in the picture in Rob's office, but so different. In the photograph, with her eyes full of laughter, she'd looked the essence of the childhood everyone craves for their sons and daughters. Today, her oval face was that of a Madonna—sad and wise before her time. Jennie guessed her age to be about fourteen. She was a smaller, more delicate version of her mother. Her hair was red-gold, a softer shade of Margaret's ginger color, and fell to her shoulders in shining ripples. She was dressed in jeans and an oversized man's shirt. Jennie thought of Tommy's penchant for wearing one of his father's shirts when upset.

Margaret took a series of shallow breaths before she spoke again. "Come on in, baby." She held out both arms.

The child crossed the room, detouring in a wide arc around Jennie's feet. The two schnauzers kept within inches of her heels, moving when she did as if attached by invisible cords.

Margaret put her arms around the girl and drew her into the chair. "Chloe, this is Mrs. Connors. She's the one who found Daddy." She looked over at Jennie. "My daughter, Chloe."

"Hello, Chloe. I'm so sorry about your father."

Chloe nodded. Her green eyes were as round as dinner plates, but there was no sign of tears.

Margaret had become calm, at least on the surface. She smoothed her daughter's hair and left her hand cupped over the dome of the small, neat head. "Mrs. Connors is going to help us see that his murderer is punished." She looked again at Jennie and articulated precisely, "Aren't you?"

Jennie attempted a smile while she tried to think of how to respond. "I'd like to help, but I'm afraid I don't know as much as you think I do. I certainly don't know who killed him."

Chloe spoke for the first time. "Dad found out Web Barrons was stealing money, and Web killed him so he wouldn't tell his father." Her voice was level, her manner chillingly calm.

"I didn't see Web or anyone else." Jennie wondered what they had been told about the night before.

"The police think my dad stole the money."

Margaret twisted in the chair so she could look into Chloe's face. "Were you listening at the door when I spoke to the lieutenant?" When her question was ignored, she added, "You know that's wrong."

"How else will I find out what's going on? You never tell me anything."

This is a family thing. I don't belong here. Jennie made a show of looking at the clock and gathered up her bag. "I should be going."

It was Chloe who stopped her. "I want to know about my dad. Did he look . . ."—she faltered for the first time, lifted her chin and went on—". . . scared?"

After a long look at her daughter, Margaret said to Jennie, "Please stay. We need to know what happened. It may sound morbid, but we do."

Jennie sat back down. "I'll tell you what I know. It isn't much. I went into Preston Barron's office. I just saw an arm. Never the whole person. But I knew something was wrong. I checked for a pulse and couldn't find one." Putting it into words brought back the horror she'd felt at the time. She paused, looked across the room, and struggled to match the calm shown by the two people staring so intently into her eyes. "I don't know if he looked scared. I didn't see his face. When I realized he was dead, I just wanted to get away. On my way out, I kicked a gun, and that's when I knew someone must have been shot."

"He was shot in the back," Margaret said, "by someone who was standing right behind him. He had no warning. No chance to get away. He died instantly."

She was looking at Jennie, but Jennie knew she was speaking to Chloe, assuring the girl that her father hadn't suffered. Was it true? Jennie had no idea. It sounded like what might have happened.

Chloe asked, "Did the police tell you that?"

"Yes." There was no hesitation in Margaret's answer.

Jennie remembered her conversation with Masoski, his asking where she'd been at midnight, and asked, "Did they tell you what time he died?"

"It was about midnight."

"I didn't get there until a little after two. That's two hours later. The killer would have gotten out of there as soon as possible. It must have been someone else I heard."

"Or the killer came back."

"That's possible. Either way, I didn't see anybody." Jennie had been prepared to face hysterics. This numb practicality was somehow worse. She fiddled with the strap of her shoulder bag, trying not to let them see that her hands were shaking.

Her distress must have shown in her face, because Margaret said, "It's okay. Chloe's right. Rob and I've always tried to shield her, but this isn't going away. She may as well hear what you have to say."

Chloe relaxed visibly. She gave her mother a hug, extracted herself from the chair they'd been sharing, and joined Jennie on the love seat.

Jennie said, "You mentioned something about Web's

stealing money. It sounded like you were going to say your dad told you about it. Did he?"

Margaret answered for her daughter. "Rob said the money from the Gala had gone missing. He said he knew who took it and that Preston knew, too."

"Did he say it was Web?"

Margaret ignored Jennie's question and leaned forward. "Rob was going to meet Preston Barrons at the bank that night." She paused, then added, "At midnight."

"Just the two of them—just Preston and Rob?"

"That's all Rob said. Even that I had to pry out of him."

"Why in the middle of the night? Didn't that seem odd to you?"

"More than odd. Frightening. I'm sure the time was Preston's idea. When I tried to talk to Rob, he told me not to worry. Said he had everything under control." She paused, studied her hands, and finally spoke again. "I can guess what happened. Rob knew that Web had made the transfer. He also knew that Preston would try to cover it up by saying someone had gotten into Web's computer. Rob wouldn't dare confront Preston unless he had proof. He knew his career with Barrons Bank and Trust would be over. He also knew that Preston would ruin his chances of getting another job in Memphis—or, for that matter, anywhere in the South—unless he could prove what he knew. Then, even if Preston fired him, he might have a chance with another bank. I think he knew something that would convince even his father that Web was guilty. He went to the bank that night to get it and arranged to meet Preston to try to work something out." She pressed a tissue to the corner of each eye.

Jennie's head was reeling. There had been no mention to her of a meeting between Preston and Rob. Why not? Equally important, why the two-hour difference in time? She looked across the room at Margaret. "You're sure about the meeting?"

"Yes."

"Could you be mistaken about the time?"

Margaret leaned forward. "My husband left the house at twenty-five minutes before twelve on a Sunday night. He is not in the habit of going out in the middle of the night, so, yes, I'm sure about the time. In fact, we argued about it. I told you I had to pry out of him where he was going."

"I heard you arguing." Chloe spoke at just above a whisper.

Margaret looked at her daughter, then back at Jennie. "I wouldn't let him leave until he told me."

Jennie studied Margaret's face. Was she telling the truth? Instinct told Jennie she was. The more she learned, the less any of it made sense. Why would Preston arrange to meet Rob at midnight and ask her to show up two hours later? And why give her the guard's schedule so she could go in undetected? Why not just tell him to let her in? She tried to compose her thoughts. She asked, "Did Rob say how he knew Web had made the transfer?"

"No, he wouldn't talk about it at all, wouldn't even admit to me it was Web, but . . . did you know that Preston sent everyone on the sixth floor home at noon on Thursday and told them not to come in on Friday?"

Jennie nodded, then asked, "Did the employees know why they were sent home?"

"Of course they did. Not that anyone came out and

said so, but everybody knew. Secrets at that bank are about as safe as at one of Chloe's slumber parties." She brushed a piece of lint from her skirt, then went on. "Rob was impossible those two days. Moody and jumpy. I think he was trying to decide what to do. Now he's dead. Murdered. And somebody's trying to make it look like he made that transfer."

Jennie glanced at Chloe.

The child seemed to be taking everything in stride.

Jennie asked Margaret, "Did you tell Lieutenant Masoski this?"

Margaret picked at the fringe on a throw pillow. Finally she said to Chloe, "Why don't you go see if Beth wants something to drink? Maybe take her a ginger ale?" When the girl balked, Margaret added, "I'll fill you in later. Promise."

Chloe seemed to consider this, then surprised Jennie by heading for the kitchen without an argument.

Maybe she's had enough.

Margaret waited for Chloe to disappear down the hall and get drinks from the fridge. When she began to speak, she kept her voice low, presumably so her words wouldn't carry to the other rooms. "You have to understand my position. I'm a stay-at-home mom. Thirty-seven years old. I have a degree in history from UT that I've never used except to tutor at Chloe's school. Other than that, I play golf and tennis. I know all the best places in Memphis for lunch. It's not going to be easy to find a job. We need every penny from Rob's pension plan, all the sick pay and vacation leave he's got coming. If I told the police what I just told you"—she paused, staring into

Jennie's eyes—"and Preston found out, how much do you think I'd get?"

Jennie didn't answer. Twenty-four hours ago, she'd have defended Preston. Today, thinking about the freeze on her own salary, the argument stuck in her throat.

Margaret went on. "I asked you here to see if you'd help me."

"You'll be better off leaving it to the police."

"They think Rob made that transfer."

"Did Lieutenant Masoski say that?"

"He didn't have to. I know what his questions meant. The police won't make waves for the Barrons family unless someone forces them to."

"I don't know what I can do."

"Just ask around. See if you can uncover the truth."

"What if the police are right? What if I find out your husband did something wrong?"

"If that happens, we'll handle it." Margaret was silent for a moment. "I understand that Web drove you home from the bank this morning."

"Yes."

"What did he have to say?"

"He spoke highly of your husband."

"Of course he did. Nobody speaks ill of the dead. Especially if they murdered them. That would be like pinning an 'I did it' sign on their chest."

Jennie didn't argue. She thought back to her ride home from the bank. "There was one thing. Web said Rob helped him cover up some mistakes. Do you know what he meant?"

"Could have been anything. The kid's a born screwup."

Margaret shifted in her chair. "Maybe Rob told him he wasn't going to cover for him anymore, and Web couldn't take it. He's not used to being told no."

Jennie considered Margaret's theory. One unwieldy piece refused to fit. She asked, "If Rob was meeting Preston, why are you so sure he was killed by Web?"

"Web must have heard about the meeting. He was scared, wanted to know what was going to happen. So he went to the bank himself and ran into Rob. They argued . . . and Web killed him."

"Why not Preston? I mean, if he's the one Rob was meeting—"

Margaret stopped Jennie with a piercing look. "I know Preston Barrons. I know how his mind works. He's ruthless, but he doesn't lose control. Web's a different story. Everybody knows the kid's a hothead. It was Web. And his father's covering for him. Not just for the murder, but stealing the money, too. Now that Rob's dead, why not blame everything on him? To someone like Preston, that makes perfect sense."

Jennie still didn't quite buy it. "Except for one thing—it doesn't answer who killed Rob. Wouldn't Preston think of that?"

"Give him time. He'll find someone to pin that on, too." She gave Jennie a grim smile. "I'd watch my back if I were you."

That had occurred to Jennie, but she didn't feel like saying so to Margaret Payton. She remembered that Leda and Preston had asked Web to drive her home because they were on their way to see Margaret. "Leda and Preston came by earlier, didn't they? Did Preston say anything about the meeting . . . or the transferred funds?"

"No. They just made what they saw as a duty call. He said he'll do anything he can to help Chloe and me get through this. He didn't mention the money. I didn't really understand what was happening until after that policeman . . . Mas . . . what's his name?"

"Lieutenant Masoski?"

"That's it. It wasn't until after he left that I figured it out."

"What do you mean?"

"The questions he asked. Questions about money. How many bank accounts do we have? How are the accounts titled? Things like that. And he wanted to know if Rob carries a laptop computer back and forth to work every day."

"Does he?"

Margaret looked at her sharply before she nodded. "I think most bankers do." She bit her lip and tugged at a stray lock of hair. "Are you going to help us?"

"I wouldn't know where to start. My connection to Preston is through his wife, through Riverview Manor. I don't know anyone at the bank. I've met some of them, but—"

"Talk to Karl Erickson. He was Rob's assistant. He may know about Rob's suspicions. Maybe he even knew about the meeting. Try Preston's secretary. That would be even better. She's worked at the bank for twenty-two years, known Web since he was a baby. If anyone knows what's going on, it's Charlotte Ellio."

Against her better judgment, Jennie said, "Give me a list of names. I'll talk to people if I get a chance."

Driving home with Margaret's list on the seat beside her, Jennie went back over every puzzling detail. Most puzzling of all was the two-hour time difference. *If only I knew what happened between midnight and 2:00 A.M.*

Chapter Eleven

Home. It had never looked so good. Jennie pulled the car into the garage, then jogged out to the mailbox. It was dark now, so she couldn't see the mail, but size and shape told her two pieces were postcards. Back in the house, she tossed most of the mail onto the counter and read the messages from her boys.

Andy's card showed an array of Native American weapons. The words were printed in block letters that ran uphill, with the signature in proud cursive. *Dad got me a tomahawk in the gift shop. Don't worry. It's not real.* Tommy's featured Earle Fraser's *The End of the Trail* sculpture. His message: *Mom, you should see this. It's 18 feet high. That's three times as tall as Dad* was written in a rounded script that marched in straight, even lines across the small space.

Jennie smiled, wondering what Tess would think of her sons' handwriting. She stuck the cards on the fridge and resisted the urge to analyze them. It seemed an invasion of their privacy. Still, she couldn't help wondering if a child's writing could predict the adult they would become.

She pushed that to the back of her mind and concentrated on a more immediate concern: her conversation with Margaret Payton.

Was Margaret right? Jennie knew that Web Barrons was spoiled, maybe irresponsible, but was he capable of murder? Or even of stealing money? Why would a twenty-year-old with seemingly unlimited resources have to steal? On the other hand, unlimited resources might be a mixed blessing, especially if it carried with it unlimited expectations. She thought back to Web's meandering statements in the car when he drove her home.

What had Rob helped Web cover up?

She tried to imagine what it would be like to have Leda and Preston for parents. Stressful, to say the least. Enough to turn a kid into a sociopath? Would they cover for him if he were? Would they even recognize the signs? Or would parental love blind them?

The questions kept circling in her head. She needed someone to talk it out with. Who?

Tess? In her career with the FBI, she must have seen a sociopath or two. And she'd had plenty of opportunity to observe Leda. She'd nailed the handwriting analysis. How much had she learned from studying the writing, and how much was the result of two years' observation? Jennie dug in her purse for the list of names Margaret had written. She studied the spiky, cramped letter formations and wondered what Tess would have to say about them.

As she stared at the paper, Jennie faced the question she'd been avoiding. Was it ethical to share her concerns about this particular situation with a resident of Riverview

Manor, any resident? Sure, her job was to make their lives as interesting as possible, but she also had a responsibility to Riverview. She couldn't do or say anything to undermine confidence in the integrity of the institution. That ruled out Tess. Also Nate, who might not have Tess's training, but intuition and a history of living by his wits had honed his people-reading skills to a razor's edge. Nor could she seek Doreen's quiet wisdom. One by one, Jennie ticked off her usual sources of enlightenment. Most were Riverview residents. This time, she couldn't share her fears with any of them. To do so would shake the foundations of their world, threaten the safe haven Riverview Manor was supposed to be. So, who?

Dr. Woodrow Samson's face floated into her consciousness. He probably knew the Barrons family better than anyone. His mother had worked as a cook for them since before Woody's birth. He'd practically grown up in their kitchen. He was the closest thing to an older brother Web had. And Woody, more than anyone Jennie knew, loved to dissect Leda. Better yet, maybe he could talk his mother into sharing a secret or two.

Jennie grabbed the phone and punched in his number. His answering machine assured her that her call was important, yada, yada.

Doesn't anyone answer the phone anymore? She listened to the rest of the spiel and left her number, along with a brief message. Two minutes later, her phone rang.

"Hey, Jen, got your message. What's up?"

"I need to talk."

"So, talk. I'm listening."

"I mean face-to-face. My head's spinning. Ideas going off in a zillion different directions."

"Because of the murder and all?"

"Yeah, if I could just talk it over with somebody, maybe I could sort it out."

"Gotcha. I'll be at Riverview tomorrow. How about—"

"Let's meet for breakfast. My treat."

"Sure. Just say when and where."

"Blue Plate, about seven?"

Jennie turned off Popular into the parking lot of the bright yellow house that was now the Blue Plate Café. The blended aromas of fresh coffee and frying bacon greeted her when she opened the door. She found Woody seated at a round table in a corner, poring over a menu with knitted brow. Clearly, breakfast was something he took seriously. Jennie was about to sit down when the front door opened again and Woody's mother walked in.

Yes! Jennie felt as if a prayer had been answered.

Even in a maid's uniform, Dorothea Samson exuded natural elegance. Like her son, she was tall and thin, with sculpted features that could be either welcoming or forbidding, depending on her mood. Her eyes swept the room and came to rest on Woody with pride that was almost tangible. She noticed Jennie and smiled a greeting as they joined Woody at the round table. "I hope you don't mind my crashing your party."

Jennie said, "Mind? Are you kidding? I'm delighted."

Woody broke in to explain. "I talked to Mom last night after you called and told her we were getting together. She wanted to come, too. Thought she might be able to help."

A waitress appeared with a carafe filled with liquid

that looked deliciously dark and smelled even better. "This is regular. Anybody want decaf?"

All shook their heads and held off on more conversation while the waitress filled their cups. She pointed to the menus and said, "Y'all just wave me down when you're ready."

Woody waggled the menu he was holding. "May as well take care of first things first."

As soon as their orders had been placed, Dorothea cut to the chase. "I know the police think Webster had something to do with that murder." She looked at Jennie as if daring her to disagree. "They're wrong. That boy could no more kill somebody than he could take off and fly."

Jennie asked, "Why do you think they suspect him?"

"Because somebody wants them to."

"What I meant is, how do you know the police think it's Web?"

"The questions they're asking."

Jennie remembered her conversation with Margaret Payton. "Rob's widow thinks the police suspect her husband of making the funds transfer." She hesitated to look at Dorothea. "You know about the transfer, don't you?"

"Of course."

"Okay, just curious. That hasn't been in the papers so far. Just the murder. I wondered if they were withholding information for some reason."

"Preston Barrons is protecting his bank, that's why. He thinks more of that bank than he does his boy."

Against all logic, Jennie felt compelled to defend Preston. "Since the money was transferred into Web's account, he's protecting his boy, too."

Dorothea lifted her sharp chin until it seemed to point accusingly at Jennie. "He's never protected that child. Expected him to be a man when he was no more than a baby."

Jennie recalled Web's remark that his father was always trying to make a man of him, but she didn't comment. She paid close attention to Dorothea, her words and her obvious conviction.

"Preston never let up. Never seemed to realize how hard the boy was trying to please him." Dorothea paused to sip her coffee. "He's a good boy. If you ask me, better than either of his parents. Softer. But he's not weak. And he's not a murderer. Or a thief." She looked Jennie defiantly in the eye, then reached over and took her purse off the vacant chair between them. She removed a square, dog-eared envelope and handed it to Jennie. "Here," she said. "He wrote me this note when he turned eighteen. Two years ago. I saved it because I knew it came from his heart."

Jennie read: *Dear Dorrie, Thanks for your card. It was the best one I got. Thanks also for all the love you've given this spoiled rich kid over the past 18 years. If I ever manage to make anything of my life, it will be because of the things I learned from you.* When she finished reading, she looked into Dorothea's unwavering gaze.

"Folks who write notes like that don't murder other folks." It was obvious from Dorothea's tone that, for her, the matter was settled.

Jennie spoke carefully. "I don't doubt what you say about his being basically good. But I have to wonder what the kind of pressure you're talking about does to a gentle person. Especially when both parents are as"—

she hesitated, searching for the right word—"disciplined as Leda and Preston. Usually there's one parent to give a cuddle when it's needed."

Dorothea flared back at her. "That child had plenty of cuddles. I fed him chocolate chip cookies in the kitchen right along with my own babies. I stuck his pictures on that big refrigerator door. I even made his momma come in and look at his drawings. I been with that family for all of my grown-up life, and they been good to me, but I stood up to them when they were too hard on that boy. I reminded them he was a little boy and he needed a pat on the head once in a while. And when they didn't tell him they loved him, I said it for them. He's not some orphan who's forced to steal money and commit murder just to get attention. I know what everybody's thinking, and I'm telling you, they're wrong." She stopped, took a deep breath, and reached for the note.

Jennie started to hand it back. Instead, prompted by impulse, she asked, "May I keep this for a couple of days?"

Dorothea looked suspicious. "Why?"

Jennie sidestepped. "I promise you'll get it back. Maybe we can use it to help him."

Dorothea drew her hand back and repeated her earlier statement. "He's a good boy. And somebody's trying to blame him for something he didn't do. I don't know why, but I'll do anything I can to help you find out." She looked at Jennie. "I've accused you before of meddling in things that didn't concern you, but this time I'm asking you to meddle."

Jennie took a minute to process this. Dorothea was an intelligent woman, one whose common sense Jennie would have staked her own life on. But there was a level of emotion in Dorothea's judgment this time that made Jennie wonder how objective she could be.

Dorothea pressed her. "Are you going to help him?"

"I want this settled as much as anybody. I'll do everything I can to see that the truth comes out."

"Nobody can ask for more." That said, Dorothea turned her attention to the cheese grits on her plate.

The rest of the meal passed with no more mention of murder.

Jennie picked it up again when they'd finished eating and settled in for an extra cup of coffee. "I went to see Margaret Payton yesterday."

Both Woody and Dorothea looked at her as if she'd just confessed to reaching into a bucket of snakes.

Woody asked, "Why'd you do that?"

"She called and asked—actually, demanded—that I come and tell her about how I found Rob's body."

Woody whistled through his teeth. "Must have been interesting."

"You don't know the half of it. Their daughter, Chloe, was there, too."

Dorothea asked, "How's she taking it?"

"Hard to tell. She impresses me as a pretty together kid." She looked at Dorothea. "Did you know the family?"

Dorothea shrugged. "Barely. They came to picnics and such that Preston had for the bank people every summer. But I can't say I really knew them. I know Preston set a lot of store in Rob."

Jennie probed. "How about Web? Do you know how he felt?"

Dorothea seemed to consider. "Now that you mention

it, I think he probably spent more time talking to Rob Payton than any of the other bank people." She nodded. "Yes, Web seemed to like him. Why?"

"Margaret is convinced Web transferred the money and killed her husband."

"Ridiculous." Dorothea slammed her cup into the saucer hard enough to elicit sidelong glances from people at nearby tables.

Jennie persisted. "She said Rob and Preston were supposed to meet at the bank that night. She thinks Web showed up and killed Rob to keep him from telling his father something."

"Her thinkin' it don't make it true." Dorothea put her elbows on the table and leaned close to Jennie. "How come you were there that time of night anyway?"

"Preston and Leda asked me to look around to see if I could figure out who transferred the money into Web's account."

Woody asked the question that was on Jennie's mind. "What was Rob doing there?"

"I wish I knew. Maybe Preston and Rob were supposed to meet, and, for some reason, Preston decided to send me instead."

Woody spoke up. "And if we knew the reason, we'd probably know what happened."

Jennie said, "That's what I'm thinking. I'm going to find out." With that, she caught the waitress's eye and signaled for the check.

As they left the restaurant, Dorothea put her hand on Jennie's shoulder. "You be careful. You're messing in dangerous business."

Jennie sent a look that said, *Aren't you the one who asked me to mess in it?*

Dorothea acknowledged the look by saying, "Web needs all the friends he can get. I hope you'll help him."

"I'll do my best."

Chapter Twelve

J ennie stood in the parking lot with Woody and watched Dorothea's car merge into the traffic on Popular. When it disappeared, she said, "Web's lucky to have a friend like your mother."

Woody said, "She's probably the only reason he's not a complete loss as a human being."

"How about you? Do you share her faith in him?"

He shrugged and headed across the pavement without comment.

Before she started the car, Jennie checked her cell phone, which she'd turned off in the restaurant. A message from Leda greeted her: "I'm calling a special meeting this morning. Eight-thirty in the conference room. It's imperative that all staff be present."

Imperative. Leda's favorite word.

By the time Jennie got to Riverview, the rest of the staff had already assembled in the conference room.

Chaplain Joe Langley sat near the head of the long table, just to Leda's right, fingering the wooden crucifix he always wore.

Jennie slipped in and sat next to Woody.

Joe broke the expectant quiet that had settled over the room. "In view of recent events, it seems appropriate to start with a prayer." His message was short and to the point, ending with a plea for comfort to Rob Payton's family.

Following a round of soft amens, Leda cleared her throat. "I called this meeting to announce that I'll be taking some time off."

Judging by the collective intake of breath around the table, everyone else was as surprised as Jennie. She, personally, could hardly remember Leda taking a *day* off, much less *some time.*

Leda went on. "I'm sure you're all aware of the . . . situation . . . involving my family. I don't think further explanation is necessary. Alice will be in charge in my absence. I know I can count on all of you to cooperate with her as you would with me." She looked around the table, making eye contact with everyone. "I'm confident that things will continue to run smoothly." Her tone left no doubt that the last statement was a command.

The sound of feet shuffling under the table and bodies shifting in chairs competed with the murmur of blended voices, all promising support. Not that anyone disliked Alice Telford or wished her ill. And, as Leda's assistant, she was the logical choice.

Alice had been Leda's closest friend since grammar school. It was a curious friendship and, at least to outsiders, a lopsided one. Both had been born into old

---

Memphis families, rich in tradition as well as more tangible assets. Beyond that, they didn't seem to have much in common. Leda, shortly after graduating from college, had married a man twenty years her senior, from a family proclaimed *suitable* by those considered qualified to pass such judgment. Alice had never married. Leda was a natural leader who wasn't afraid to make hard choices—or to step on toes. Alice was a peacemaker, a rule follower, who'd see the world in ashes before she'd hurt anyone's feelings. People respected Leda. People genuinely liked Alice.

Leda adjusted her rimless glasses and cleared her throat, stilling the shifting and shuffling. "Alice, have you anything to say?"

Alice remained seated. "Not really. I'd just like to thank everyone in advance for their help." She smiled at each of them. "I don't anticipate any problems. You're all very good at your jobs." Her voice was little more than a whisper.

Leda nodded approvingly. "I'm confident that this matter will be settled and everything back to normal in no time."

Jennie watched Leda, noting body language that contradicted her words. There was a clenching and unclenching of fingers that wasn't typical of Riverview's Executive Director.

Leda looked imperiously around the table. "Questions?"

When no one else spoke up, Jennie said, "Not a question, but I need to talk to you." She looked around the table, then added, "It doesn't concern the rest of the group."

Leda scanned faces again. "Anyone else?"

No response.

"Then I guess we're finished here. I hope to be seeing all of you soon."

Everyone left except Leda, Alice, and Jennie.

Alice looked from Jennie to Leda. "Is this something I should be a part of?"

"No." Jennie kept her answer short. She followed Alice to the door and closed it behind her. Determined not to be intimidated, she remained standing as she faced Leda. "Margaret Payton called yesterday afternoon and asked me to visit her. She insisted that I tell her the details of how I found Rob's body."

"That must have been unpleasant." Leda's expression was noncommittal, her tone level.

Jennie swallowed her anger and matched Leda's civilized manner. "It was," she said. "She also told me that Rob was meeting Preston at the bank Sunday night. Did you know about that?"

Leda didn't answer, but a slight narrowing of her eyes told Jennie she did.

"Everything you told me was a lie." Jennie heard her voice spiraling, felt her anger threatening to take over.

Leda motioned to a chair. "Sit down. Let me explain."

"I don't want an explanation. I want the truth." Jennie approached but did not sit. She gripped a chair back and glared at the woman facing her across the table.

Leda's composure didn't slip. "I admit we weren't completely straightforward with you." She waved to the chair again. "If you calm down, we'll discuss it."

"How can you expect me to be calm? I'm probably lucky to be alive. Have you thought about that?"

"Yes. Preston and I both have. We discussed it at

length. We had no idea we were sending you into a dangerous situation."

"Well, what *did* you think you were sending me into?"

Leda put her elbows on the table and covered her face with her hands.

Jennie watched and waited, trying to remember if she'd ever seen any sign of weakness from Leda before.

After what seemed hours, Leda looked up. "It's an impossible tangle." She looked and sounded bone-weary.

Jennie didn't relent. "I deserve the truth. And if you don't tell me, I'll find it some other way. When I talked to Margaret . . ." She faltered, considered, and decided not to mention Margaret's conviction that Web had murdered Rob. She didn't want to jeopardize Margaret and Chloe's financial security—or her own, for that matter.

Leda leaned forward. "Yes?"

Jennie chose her words carefully. "She said Rob and Preston were going to meet at midnight. . . ."

Leda looked surprised. "Midnight?"

"Yes."

"That's not accurate. I've already admitted that Preston was supposed to meet Rob, but the meeting was set for two A.M."

Jennie tried to process this. "Are you sure?"

"Positive."

Leda's posture and intonation convinced Jennie she was telling the truth, or at least what she thought was the truth. *So, why—?* Jennie said, "Ever since I talked to Margaret, I've been wondering why Preston asked me to go to the bank at two . . . actually, why he sent me at all . . . but especially two hours after he was supposed to meet Rob. It doesn't make sense." She hesitated, giving

Leda time to explain. When Leda didn't, Jennie added, "Frankly, I can't come up with a single reason."

Leda silenced her by holding up a hand. "Just listen. I'll tell you the whole story, but you have to let me finish." She held Jennie's gaze for long moment. "Agreed?"

"Okay."

Leda folded her hands as if for prayer and lay them on the tabletop. "I'll begin with Preston's informing me that the Gala funds were missing. He called late Wednesday, asked if I'd taken the money out of the Special Account. I said I hadn't. He told me it was gone and asked if someone at Riverview might have transferred the funds. At that point we didn't think the money was stolen, just moved to another account or something. I told him it wasn't possible. He said it was an electronic transfer; he'd have their IT person look into it."

"Who's their IT person?"

"Karl Erickson." Leda wagged a finger at Jennie. "You agreed to let me tell the story without interruptions."

Jennie nodded.

Leda continued, "He called back a little later. Upset. Asked if I was alone. I told him I was. He informed me the money was in our son's personal account and that the transfer had been made using Web's laptop computer. I was shocked, of course." She leaned toward Jennie. "I want you to know that neither Preston nor I ever for one minute believed Web had stolen that money. Our faith in our son is unshakable." When Jennie didn't comment, she went on. "That little scene you witnessed between Web and his father yesterday morning . . . that was merely normal father-son tension . . . well, perhaps a bit more than that, but it has nothing to do with the Gala funds." She gazed into space, then went on. "Preston became a father late in life, and he sometimes has trouble understanding young people. He's always had his heart set on Web's following him into the bank, carrying on the family tradition."

Jennie prompted, "You still haven't told me why I was sent to the bank, particularly at that time."

Leda removed her glasses and let them hang from the chain around her neck. "You already know that Preston, after much agonizing, gave the employees on the sixth floor some time off. He felt certain—still does, actually—that one of them had made the transfer. He determined to search their work spaces for evidence of who it was. I tried to talk him out of it, but he wouldn't listen. He didn't find anything, but he wasn't ready to give up. I suggested he ask you to help. That much is true. Our original plan was to ask you to accompany Preston and me to the bank, and, together, you and he could search the work spaces again. Then, out of the blue, Rob called and told Preston he was pretty sure he knew who was responsible for the transfer. When Preston tried to get a name, Rob was evasive—said he didn't want to do that until he was one hundred percent sure. He's the one who suggested the time of the meeting. The whole thing seemed like a bad idea to me. Again, I tried to talk Preston out of it. He refused to listen."

Jennie knew she'd agreed to let Leda speak without interruption, but she couldn't stop herself. "So you knew it was dangerous."

"I didn't think it could be deadly. My fear was that Preston, when he discovered who had tried to frame our son, would become upset and do or say something irrational."

"Like what?"

"I don't know. I didn't have anything specific in mind. I was nervous about the whole setup. You have to remember we were concerned about Web. We—and I mean both Preston and I—weren't thinking clearly."

"I still don't understand why you sent me."

"I finally persuaded Preston that he, as president of the bank, should not be a part of any meeting, that if he were involved, it might actually make it look worse for Web. I suggested you because you have a knack for dealing with difficult people. I thought you might be able to persuade Rob to tell you who had taken the money. Then you could relay the information to Preston, and he could deal with it."

"Why didn't you tell me the truth?"

"What we told you was very close to the truth."

Jennie thought over Leda's explanation. It sounded very much like the stories her boys came up with when they were pushed into a corner—true except for one glaring omission. "Why didn't you tell me Rob would be there? Didn't you think I should be prepared for that?"

Leda sighed. "In hindsight, yes, it was foolish, but we were afraid you wouldn't agree."

"Did Rob know I was coming in Preston's place?"

"No. We were afraid Rob would cancel. We were sure you'd work it out."

Unbelievable.

The two women stared at each other. Leda actually looked embarrassed—a first in Jennie's experience.

There was still one major sore point to address. Jennie

took a deep breath. "So you came up with the idea to freeze my salary. The deal clincher."

Leda met Jennie's gaze. "We did not *come up* with the idea. Once the account was violated, Preston had no choice. It's his duty to protect the remaining funds. Unfortunately—"

Jennie didn't let her finish. "It just so happened I wouldn't get paid. So I had no choice either."

"Jennifer, believe me, I . . . neither Preston nor I . . . want to hurt you in any way. Surely, you realize that." She opened a drawer and removed a checkbook, which she lay on the desk. "I personally will—"

"I'll be fine." It wasn't quite true, but Jennie would follow a pretty slim diet before she'd accept money from Leda.

Leda looked ready to insist when they were interrupted by a commotion in the hall. Nate's mellifluous voice rose, clear and unmistakable, above the babble of half a dozen others.

Jennie rose, ready to do what she could to restore order.

Leda lay her hand on Jennie's arm. "I'm counting on you to keep the peace. Alice can handle the administrative details, but . . ." She looked meaningfully toward the door leading to the hall. "The residents need you, especially . . ." She tilted her head toward the escalating argument outside the door.

Chapter Thirteen

When Jennie entered the hall, the argument was at a standoff. Literally.

Nate posed in the center of the corridor, chin high, shoulders squared—his me-against-the-world stance. "The real problem here is small-mindedness." He spoke in his plummiest stage voice, choosing disdain as the emotion of the moment.

Jennie listened for the message behind the words. She'd defended the old actor often enough to make the translation easily: *Small-mindedness. Means he knows he's wrong but doesn't intend to back down.*

Mr. Appleton stood five feet from Nate, considerably less dramatic but no less determined. "Frankly, I don't care what you think of the size of my mind. My daughter knitted that sweater for me, and I want it back." He was a small man, potbellied, who didn't mix much with the other residents. He'd only been at Riverview for two weeks, and this was his first brush with Nate. Jennie hadn't had a chance to get to know him yet, though she'd made every effort.

He drew himself up and stepped closer to Nate. "Give. Me. My. Sweater."

Jennie stepped between them.

Georgie Peterson stood off to one side. Her mischievous gaze darted from one combatant to the other, ready—Jennie knew from experience—to add fuel should the fire threaten to go out.

From the corner of her eye, Jennie saw Alice duck back into her office. *Leda's right. Alice can't deal with conflict.*

Jennie knew that what Nate loved most was undivided attention, so she ignored him and focused on Mr. Appleton. "Your daughter knitted this?" She faced Nate but looked only at the sweater, ignoring its wearer. "This pattern . . . it's so intricate. And the buttons . . ." She rubbed her fingers over one of the small disks—"What kind of wood is that?"—and spoke over her shoulder in Mr. Appleton's direction. "Do you know?"

"Walnut. My son-in-law's a cabinetmaker. He makes buttons for Lizzie's projects from his scraps." There was no missing the pride in his voice.

Taking their cue from Jennie, other residents edged closer. There was much oohing and aahing over the buttons. No one looked at Nate.

Jennie heard a wicked giggle in the background that could only come from Georgie.

"Humph." Nate removed the sweater, presented it to Jennie with a grandiose gesture, then turned and stalked away, heels clicking, head held high.

Jennie tucked the garment around Mr. Appleton's

shoulders. "Nate doesn't mean any harm. He just likes to test new people." When there was no response, she added, "I hope to meet your daughter soon. Your son-in-law, too. They sound like interesting people."

"They are." He favored her with a tentative smile.

Jennie thought maybe Nate had given her the entrée she needed to break through Mr. Appleton's reserve, but before she had a chance to pursue it, the newcomer mumbled something about having a letter to write and hurried away with his fingers curled protectively around the sweater. Jennie wasn't discouraged. She knew her time would come.

That pleasant thought was cut short when Alice reappeared and said, "Jennie, Tess is looking for you."

Jennie headed for Tess's room with less than her usual enthusiasm. She was pretty sure she knew what Tess wanted. Since she'd already decided it was unethical to discuss the funds transfer or the murder with Riverview's residents, she braced for another ticklish situation. When she reached Tess's door, she paused at the threshold, stood at attention, and saluted. "You looking for me?"

Tess chuckled and saluted back. "I was beginning to think you were avoiding me."

"Never." Jennie came the rest of the way into the room. "I haven't had time to visit with anyone. Leda called a staff meeting this morning. Then, when that was over, I ran into a little set-to in the hall."

"I heard the voices," Tess said. "Figured Nate was up to his usual tricks."

"You figured right."

Tess regarded Jennie with a half smile, seemingly waiting for more.

Jennie smiled back but said nothing.

Tess held up the folder containing the photocopies they'd made the day before. "I've been looking over these."

"Oh." Jennie reached for the folder. "This investigating business probably isn't a good idea."

Tess's mouth settled into a straight line. "Why not?" She did not relinquish her hold on the folder.

Jennie's hand was still extended toward the folder when her cell phone rang. She directed an apologetic grin toward Tess before she checked caller ID. Her heart did a quick flip. "I have to answer. It's my kids."

"Of course." Tess tactfully turned toward the window, where a hummingbird hovered near a trumpet vine.

Jennie answered the phone and heard Tom's voice: "Hi. We're just checking in before we go on a trail ride. Everyone's fine here."

"Where are you?"

"Haunted Trails Campground. It's close to Flagstaff." His voice drifted, as though he'd turned his head away. "Okay, okay." It grew strong again. "Here's Andy."

"Guess what, Mom?"

Savoring the lilt of his words, Jennie entered the spirit of the game. "How about a hint?"

"I lost something."

"Hope it wasn't your sunscreen."

"Not even close. Another tooth. Yesterday."

"Did the tooth fairy find you way out there?"

"Mom." His world-weary tone said a lot more than the single word.

Jennie rephrased her question. "Well, did you get any money for the tooth?"

"Not at first. It got lost in my sleeping bag." He stopped to laugh. "Then Dad looked for the tooth, and he found a dollar in there, too."

"So, maybe the tooth fairy has a cousin who lives in the desert."

"Yeah, right."

"Anyway, Dad said you're about to go on a trail ride. Sounds like fun."

"Yeah, the leader's a real cowboy. You should see his hat."

"Good-looking hat?"

"Just the opposite. It's all beat up. He said it's probably older than I am."

"An antique, huh?"

"Yeah, kinda." There was a pause, then: "Tommy wants to talk, too."

Tommy came on. "Hi, Mom. You okay?"

"I miss you and Andy. Other than that, I'm great."

"We miss you, too." There was a pause, the sound of soft breathing.

Jennie recognized the tug children of divorce feel when sandwiched between competing loyalties and adopted a more upbeat tone. "That's sweet, but I'm really glad you guys are having a good time." A lump in her throat made her hesitate. "Keep safe. Remember there are all kinds of dangers in the desert. Different things than you're used to around here."

"Don't worry. Dad's taking good care of us. And this cowboy guy, too . . . his name's Devon. You ever hear of a cowboy named Devon?"

Laughter replaced the lump in her throat. "I don't think so."

"Me neither . . . Dad wants to talk to you again."

"Okay, love you."

"Love you, too."

She heard the phone being handed off, then Tom's voice: "Me again."

Raucous laughter in the background prompted her to say, "Sounds like the kids're having fun."

"They are. Enough about that." There was a pause. The laughter grew less distinct. Jennie pictured Tom stepping away to say something he didn't want the kids to hear. When he spoke, his voice was lower—so soft, she had trouble making out his words. "What happened with your cloak-and-dagger trip to the bank? Obviously you survived it."

She considered letting it go at that, but long habit of confiding in Tom won out. "Barely. Preston's right-hand man was murdered, and I stumbled over the body."

Tom groaned.

"It's not that bad. I turned everything over to the police, and I'm out of it."

"What do you mean? What did you turn over to the police?"

She realized she should have chosen her words more carefully. "There were some papers."

"What kind of papers?"

"I'm not sure. They might have something to do with a motive."

"Why did you have them in the first place?"

This was getting annoying. Jennie reminded herself they weren't married anymore. "Don't worry about it. Like I said, I'm out of it. Enjoy your trail ride. Hug the kids for me. Bye."

She started to snap the phone closed and saw she had a text message. She stared at the number but didn't recognize it. *Wonder who . . .* She pushed more buttons.

Nobody likes a busybody, the message read.

She ignored the prickling at the back of her neck and turned off the phone. She forced herself to recall the unfamiliar number and said it softly to herself until she was reasonably sure she had it right.

Tess was watching through narrowed eyes.

Jennie said, "I'd love to stay and chat, but I have some things to take care of."

The former FBI agent wasn't easily put off. "What's up?"

"Nothing." Jennie could almost see the wheels turning in the old pro's head. She slipped the phone into her pocket and broadened her smile until she felt her face would crack. "Why?"

The older woman kept her level gaze on Jennie's face. "Someone left a nasty message for you, didn't they?" When Jennie didn't answer, she added, "Never take a threat lightly."

"It wasn't a threat." *Was it?* "Why do you think that?"

A lift of her shoulders was Tess's only reply.

Jennie said, "You shouldn't be involved in this. Neither should I. I'm going to let the police handle it."

"You've decided not to worry me." Tess cocked her head to one side. "Right?"

"Something like that."

Tess leaned forward and peered over her glasses. "I expect better of you, Jennie."

Jennie opened her mouth.

Tess cut her off. "Most of the time I'd agree that a homicide is best left to the police, but, like it or not, you're involved." She removed the glasses and pointed them in Jennie's direction. "If I know you as well as I think I do, you won't stay out of it . . . or ask for help. You'll try to go it alone out of the misguided notion you're protecting us residents by leaving us in the dark." She jabbed the air with the glasses. "That's ridiculous! Nobody is better off in the dark. I can help. I have a lot more experience than that police lieutenant."

"I won't argue with that." Jennie met Tess's gaze and resisted the urge to back down. When Tess didn't back down either, Jennie said, "I have to go."

Tess grabbed Jennie's arm as she turned. "I saw your face when you read that message. Something about it bothered you. If you don't want to tell me what it was, I can't make you." Her fingers gripped harder. "But there's one thing I want you to remember. The first murder is the hardest. Once a person crosses that line, they have nothing to lose by killing again."

Chapter Fourteen

Jennie hurried to her office and grabbed a pen. She closed her eyes and forced herself to see the digits that had appeared in the window before she'd retrieved the text message. She looked at the number she'd written. *I'm sure that's right.*

She'd give it to Masoski later. Right now, she wanted to talk to a couple of people. She dialed Barrons Bank and Trust Company. When a polite voice answered, she asked for Charlotte Ellio.

Forty-five minutes later, she was standing beside the customer service desk of the bank, waiting for Preston Barrons' secretary to join her for lunch. She studied the bustle of lunchtime activity and reflected that news of a murder on the premises didn't seem to hurt business. It was 12:30, and the lobby was full. All the tellers' windows were staffed and had lines snaking into the open space. Customers' attire ran the gamut from businessmen in suits and ties to a trio of teenaged girls in hip-hugging jeans and skimpy T-shirts. Jennie was somewhere in the middle with her gauzy yellow sundress and sandals. A few customers chatted as they waited. Others tapped their feet and glanced at their watches.

Several people greeted Charlotte when she crossed the lobby to where Jennie waited. She didn't acknowledge them but kept her eyes on Jennie. Her expression was grim, a far cry from the composed woman Jennie had met yesterday morning.

This isn't going to be easy. Jennie smiled and extended her hand.

Charlotte accepted the hand but didn't return the smile. Her auburn hair stood out in tufts above her ears. Her skirt was awry, her royal blue silk blouse half in, half out. Something was clearly wrong. "I have to cancel our lunch date."

Jennie felt rotten about it, but she persisted. "If not lunch, how about a few minutes of your time?" When the other woman didn't respond, she added, "A couple of minutes. That's all I'm asking."

Charlotte sighed. "I'm not trying to put you off. I have to take care of something."

Preston Barrons exited the elevator, hesitated when he saw Jennie and his secretary talking, then nodded. Jennie noted that he darted a curious look over his shoulder before he went out into the street.

Charlotte stared after him. "I have to get back upstairs." She shifted from one foot to the other like a toddler postponing a trip to the bathroom.

Jennie refused to give up. "Margaret Payton asked me to talk to you."

That got a reaction. The restless movements ceased, but the furrows in her forehead grew deeper. "Why me?"

"Margaret said if anyone knows what's going on, you do." A subtle change in expression told Jennie she had Charlotte's attention. "Maybe we can go somewhere a little more private." She looked around the crowded lobby.

Marble floors and paneled walls bounced back sounds and mixed them, but one or two voices remained distinct; stray bits of conversation were distinguishable in the general dissonance.

"Tell you what," Charlotte said. "I don't have time to go out for lunch, but you're welcome to come with me while I get something from the machines."

"Sure." Jennie was more than willing. She tagged along when Charlotte turned and headed toward the elevator.

Two women carrying white paper bags redolent of fried onions rode up with them. "Good morning, Mrs. Ellio," they said, almost in unison.

She answered with a mechanical smile.

Jennie took her silence as a cue and held off on the questions she wanted to ask.

They got off on the third floor, turned left, and entered a square room with a high ceiling from which metal lighting fixtures hung on chains. Vertical blinds kept out natural light while fluorescent bulbs cast a cold bluish wash over the tiled floor and dingy, unadorned walls. Square tables, surrounded by metal folding chairs, were clustered in front of a row of vending machines. The room was nothing like the luxurious lobby that greeted customers. The only attempt at décor was an arrangement of plastic flowers on each table. It was not enough.

Charlotte approached a machine, then stopped. "I left my purse upstairs."

Jennie said, "Let me get it. I invited you to lunch. I had something a little more upscale in mind, but—"

"I have to check something. If you don't mind waiting, we'll talk when I get back."

"I don't mind," Jennie said. What choice did she have?

Only three tables were occupied. Jennie headed toward a spot in a corner. It looked like the best bet for a private conversation. She sat down, wondering if anyone knew she was the person who had discovered their fellow employee's body just a couple of nights ago. If they did, they didn't show it. They went on with their conversations, casting an occasional glance in her direction.

When Charlotte came back, her mood had lifted. She nodded at everyone. Her face brightened when she spotted a young man at one table. She said, "Hi, Eddie, how's the new baby?" but didn't slow down to hear his response. She went to the bank of vending machines, turned to Jennie, and said, "Getting anything?"

Jennie nodded and joined her in front of the machines. "Any recommendations?"

Charlotte fed a five-dollar bill into a narrow slot. "Believe it or not, the ham sandwiches aren't too bad." She removed a plastic-wrapped bundle, scooped out her change, and stepped sideways to the Snapple dispenser.

Jennie settled on apple juice and peanut butter crackers. "Did you fix your problem?" she asked when they were seated.

"I beg your pardon?"

"You said you had to check something upstairs. You seemed upset. You don't seem upset anymore, so . . ."

"You're right. I was pretty rattled when I came down." Charlotte paused to bite into her sandwich, and when she'd swallowed, she said, "I did something dumb this morning, but then I realized how to take care of it." She smiled at Jennie for the first time. "You say Margaret Payton asked you to talk to me?" Charlotte pronounced the words casually, but her hands shook as she twisted the top off the Snapple.

"Yes. She claims her husband knew who transferred the money into Web's account. And she's convinced that whoever it was found out he knew and killed him."

"Did she say who?"

"She doesn't know. Rob wouldn't tell her."

Charlotte sipped her drink. "The police seem to think Rob took the money."

"They gave Margaret that impression, too." Jennie watched Charlotte's face as she asked the next question. "What do you think?"

Charlotte glanced toward the other tables before she leaned forward and whispered, "I think Web did it himself. Rob found out and tried to help him out of a jam."

"But why?"

"Rob took Web under his wing. Said the kid needed a break. Personally, I think he's had nothing but good breaks his whole life."

Jennie tried again. "I meant, why would Web have to steal money?"

"God only knows."

"Okay. Suppose he did. Does that mean he killed Rob?"

"Probably." Charlotte's grim smile and curt nod hinted at satisfaction in believing Web was a criminal. *She doesn't like him.* "Did you tell the police what you think? About Web, I mean?"

Something caught Charlotte's attention. She sat up straight and didn't answer.

Jennie glanced over and saw a young man gliding toward them. Tall. Blond. Killer smile. Jennie knew she'd seen him before but took a few seconds to place him as Karl Erickson, the late Rob Payton's assistant. The fact that she'd almost forgotten him showed how upset she'd been. He was, to borrow a phrase from her grandmother, handsome as the devil on horseback. When he reached their table, he cupped his hand on Charlotte's shoulder. "Hear you had a little problem this morning."

There was an almost imperceptible flinching at his touch. "It's been taken care of." Her tone was cordial— barely.

She doesn't like this guy any better than she does Web.

Erickson seemed impervious to the cool reception. He pulled up a chair and joined them. When Charlotte refused to look at him or speak again, he stretched out his hand to Jennie. "I'm Karl."

Jennie met his hand halfway. "Jennie Connors. We met yesterday."

He flashed that smile, and Jennie added perfect teeth to his list of attributes.

"I remember," he said. "You're the lady the boss gave the key to the bank to."

Jennie wasn't sure if she should be flattered or offended by the suggestive way he'd said that. Then he smiled again, and she was definitely flattered. Before she could think of an appropriate response, a skeletally thin man in baggy khakis approached. The area around his eyes was a mass of crinkly lines. Other than that, he looked young.

Karl said, "Hi, Roger."

Charlotte half rose, smiling expectantly. "Any luck?"

Roger shook his head. "It's gone." The lines around his eyes deepened.

Charlotte dropped back into her chair. Her smile disappeared. "Are you sure?"

He hunched his shoulders and spread his hands. "I looked everywhere."

Karl watched and finally spoke. "You talking about the backup?"

Roger nodded.

Charlotte's face was a mask.

Karl said, "I might be able to do something."

Charlotte shook her head and looked at the other man. "It has to be there. You must have missed it." She glanced at Jennie but did not look in Karl's direction.

Roger stood twisting his hands as though washing them.

Karl's glance darted from Roger to Charlotte, then back to Roger. "I'll help you look," he said, and he rose from his chair. He put his hand on the other man's shoulder, and they left together.

Jennie heard Roger say, "You're wasting your time," as they walked toward the elevator.

Charlotte stared after them.

"What kind of backup is it?" Jennie asked.

Charlotte nibbled at her sandwich, then covered it with

a napkin and pushed it away. "This morning, right after I came in . . . I'd just turned on my computer . . . I don't know what I did, but I deleted some files off my hard drive." She sipped her tea. "Unfortunately, they were all personal files and not on the network computer." She leaned forward, put her elbows on the table, and rested her face in her hands. When she looked up, her expression was unreadable.

Jennie said, "You have personal files on your work computer?"

"What I meant is that they were files related to things I take care of for Preston. They're not on any computer except mine."

"Ouch."

"Exactly."

Jennie tried to reassure her. "Karl said he might be able to help."

"He'd love that. He'd be the guy on the white horse, and I'd be so grateful, I wouldn't yell when he started hitting on my daughter." She drained the Snapple and set the bottle on the table with a thud. "Or so he thinks."

Aha! "How old is your daughter?"

"Just turned seventeen."

"How old's Karl?"

"Twenty-four." She tore a jagged gash in the Snapple label. "Too old for Wendy."

And much too handsome for a seventeen-year-old to ignore. Aloud, she said, "You never did say if you told the police you think Web transferred the money."

Charlotte gave her a sidelong look. "His father's my boss. What do you think?"

Jennie wanted to be sure. "You're afraid you might lose your job if you say anything against Web?"

"No 'might' about it. It's a sure thing. And I'm not going to let that happen. My daughter has one more year of high school. We're looking at colleges. It won't be easy, but she's going to have her chance—even if it means a spoiled rich kid gets away with murder."

Chapter Fifteen

When Charlotte headed back to her office, Jennie traipsed along. She wasn't invited, but, on the other hand, no one told her to leave. She stayed close to Charlotte and tried to be invisible. One person to whom she was obviously not invisible was Karl Erickson. He was hunched over a bank of file cabinets just outside Charlotte's door and caught Jennie's eye with a mischievous grin when she brushed past.

Jeez, he's good-looking. Twenty-four's kind of young, though. Did he really hit on Charlotte's daughter?

Charlotte glanced in Karl's direction and muttered something under her breath that Jennie didn't catch. In deference to Charlotte, Jennie put on a poker face. She reminded herself of her own age—thirty-one. *Yeah, he's too young. But why? Tom's nine years older than me, and nobody thought that was so bad.* She let her smile shine in Karl's direction. *Sauce for the goose!*

Charlotte was settling into her chair when Roger

poked his head in. "I still can't find that backup. The old ones are in the cabinet, but not the latest."

Karl took a sidestep that placed him in the center of the door opening. "I looked, too, and the most current backup for your computer is two weeks old."

There was dead silence.

Karl turned to Roger. "What about recent backups for the other computers?"

"Everything else is there." Roger paused, then stooped to pick up something. "This yours?" He held out a clip-on earring, a cloisonné oval that matched the blue of Charlotte's blouse.

She reached for the earring but didn't put it on. Instead she placed it on her desk, next to the phone. "Thanks." She shoved some papers into a wire basket.

Jennie noticed a cell phone in the basket, apparently used as a paperweight. *Does she always leave it there? Where anyone can get to it?* She glanced at Charlotte, surprised at her composed expression. *She doesn't seem worried about the files. She was sure upset before though. Maybe she doesn't want Karl to know they're important.*

Roger and Karl exchanged coded looks behind Charlotte's back.

Jennie wondered what they meant. A vibration in her pocket distracted her. She checked caller ID. *Riverview. Have to take that.* She excused herself and stepped away. "Hello."

"Jennie, where are you?" It wasn't like Alice to be so abrupt.

"At the bank. I had a lunch date with Charlotte Ellio. Thought I told you."

Alice sighed. "Yes, I guess you did." Another sigh, a

huge one. "Are you finished? Can you get back here by two-thirty?"

Jennie glanced at her watch. 2:07. "I guess so. What's wrong?"

"Nothing's wrong. I need you to do something, that's all."

"What is it?"

"A reporter from the *Commercial Appeal* called. She wants to do a piece on our Fourth of July celebration." Alice's normally calm tone ascended to a squeak. "She'll be here at two-thirty."

"You're in charge now. You're the one she wants to talk to."

"But the celebration and the Gala have always been tied together. What if she asks about the Gala moncy? Or thc murder?"

"Tell her you don't know anything. The police are still investigating. Smile a lot and show her around. Offer to take her out to the island."

"I want you to handle it."

Grow up, Alice. Aloud, Jennie said, "I'm leaving now. It shouldn't take more than twenty minutes." She slipped the phone back into her pocket and returned to the threesome staring at Charlotte's monitor. She caught Charlotte's eye. "I have to go. Thanks for seeing me." She started to leave, changed her mind, and spoke to Charlotte again. "We didn't get to talk much. Mind if I call later, maybe this evening?"

"That'd be fine," she agreed without looking up from the lines flitting by on her screen.

"Want to give me your cell phone number?"

Charlotte focused on Jennie now. After a moment's

hesitation, she scribbled something on a slip of paper and handed it to her. "Here's my home number." Her eyes strayed to the phone in the basket. "I only use the cell to talk to my daughter. I refuse to be one of those people who walk around with a phone glued to their ear."

"I know what you mean," Jennie said, but she couldn't help wondering if there was more to it than that. "Thanks again. Maybe sometime we can go out for a real lunch."

"Maybe." Charlotte's *maybe* sounded like a definite *no*.

Karl dashed up and thrust his hand out to stop the elevator door from closing. He flashed that killer smile and stepped in. "Am I next?"

Jennie laughed out loud. It was impossible not to respond to his good humor. "Next for what?"

"If I'm not on your list of folks to question, my feelings are going to be hurt."

"What makes you think I have a list?"

"Well . . ."—he stretched the word out in a charming drawl—"I've never seen you around here before. The only reason I can think of for you to be here now is to check out possible suspects for your boss, who just happens to be *my* boss's wife."

They were standing side by side, facing the metal doors. Karl tilted his head and looked into her eyes. "I've already been questioned by Lieutenant Masoski. I'd much rather tell my story to you. I have one condition, though." That smile was not easy to resist.

Jennie didn't try too hard. "Oh?"

"Let's find an interesting locale."

"Such as?"

"How about Southland?"

"Pardon?"

"Guess you're not a racing fan."

"You talking about the dog track over in Arkansas?"

"I am. You a fan?"

"I don't know. We used to go up to Louisville for the horse races a couple times a year, but I've never been to a dog race."

"We need to remedy that. By the way, who's the other part of 'we'?"

"I went with my husband . . . my ex now."

The smile widened. After a brief, quiet moment during which he looked into Jennie's eyes, Karl said, "If you like horse races, you'll like dog races. Argh!" He stopped, spun around on his heel, and slapped his forehead. "Today's Tuesday, right?"

His expression reminded Jennie of Andy at homework time. She was totally charmed. "Let me guess. No races on Tuesday?"

"Not live. Just simulcast." His face brightened. "It's still a fun place to go. Especially if you have somebody to introduce you to all the interesting characters."

The elevator doors opened. Jennie and Karl moved closer together as they stepped into the crowded lobby.

"You know all the interesting characters?"

"Most of them. So, how about it? You ready to broaden your circle of acquaintances?"

"Sure." Jennie told herself that meeting with Karl was not a date. Margaret Payton had asked her to talk to him. That's why she was going. Sure, it was. The fact that he was handsome as sin had nothing to do with it.

He went outside with her. Heat rose from the sidewalk

in shimmers, oppressive after the bank's cool interior. Jennie glanced up at a building with a sign displaying the time and temperature. Ninety-seven degrees. The time was 2:13.

Karl wiped his brow. "Maybe an air-conditioned bar would be better."

"Oh, no, you promised to introduce me to some interesting characters."

"That I did. First race is seven-thirty. Pick you up around seven?"

"I have to go back to work now. I'm not sure when I'll get away. I'll meet you at the track."

"Okay." He started to go in, then turned and asked, "You know where it is?"

"Just across the bridge, right?"

"You got it." She glanced at the time display again as she started toward the parking garage. It was now 2:16. *By the time I get to my car . . . It'll be close.*

On the drive back, she went over the aborted lunch date with Charlotte. Had she learned anything useful? What was the significance of the lost files? Did they relate to the funds transfer? If so, they must also be tied to Rob Payton's death. On a more personal level, had Charlotte sent that text message? If not, why wouldn't she give out her cell phone number? And what about Karl Erickson? *Guess I'll find out about* him *tonight.*

Jennie glanced at the dash when she pulled into Riverview's parking lot. 2:43. *Maybe the reporter's late.*

No such luck. Jennie went directly to the Activities Room and found Alice and a petite brunet waiting for her. They were standing in front of the French doors, looking out into the enclosed courtyard. Jennie took a moment to study them.

The brunet was wearing a sleeveless linen shift in an icy shade of blue. Her shoes had the highest, thinnest heels Jennie had ever seen. *More interested in style than comfort.* She pondered how this should affect her approach to the interview. "Hi. Sorry I'm late."

The two women turned simultaneously when Jennie spoke. The brunet, who looked about twenty-five, stepped forward and extended her hand. "Brooke Newton."

Alice remained two steps behind, smiling nervously.

"Jennie Connors." Jennie accepted the proffered hand. "Any relation to Jill Newton, the TV reporter?"

"We're sisters."

"Nice to meet you. I've crossed paths with Jill a couple of times."

"So I've heard."

Her tone made Jennie wonder exactly *what* she had heard. *Probably best not to think about that.* "So, news is the family game."

"I guess you could say that."

Alice slipped from the room during the exchange of small talk.

Jennie gestured to a chair. "I understand you want to write about our fireworks display. What do you want to know?"

Brooke sat down and pulled a notebook and a pen from her bag. "You can start by telling me something about the history of your celebration."

"Most of our residents are patriotic, especially the World War II vets. The Fourth of July's a major holiday to them, but, since it's summer, a lot of their kids and grandkids are busy with other things and—" A tapping toe distracted Jennie. She paused to analyze the polite look on her listener's face. "I'm boring you."

A flush crept over Brooke's cheeks. "No, you're not."

"Yeah, I am. Why don't you ask questions, and I'll try to keep my answers short." Jennie paused for a quick laugh. "I'm one of those rare birds who loves her job. When I talk about it, I have a tendency to run off at the mouth." She folded her hands in her lap. "Fire away."

"Okay." Brooke's eyes narrowed ever so slightly and lost the bored look. "What I think is really interesting is the tie-in between your Gala and the Fourth of July celebration. I'd like to hear about both of them."

The hairs on the back of Jennie's neck began to tickle. *The Gala. Alice was right.* She spoke slowly, determined to make the reporter see the good things about Riverview Manor and its celebrations. "The last Saturday in June, we host a fund-raiser. It's a big deal, makes a lot of money, mostly due to Leda Barrons. She calls in favors and twists the arms of all her friends so—"

Brooke scribbled away.

Jennie reached toward the hand that held the pen. "I don't mean that in a bad way. What I mean is, Leda knows a lot of people, and most of them are generous. So the Gala brings in quite a bit of money."

"Don't worry, I won't make you look bad to your boss." Brooke flashed a conspirator's grin at Jennie. "What happens to the money?"

Alarms were sounding in Jennie's head. She chose her words with care. "It goes into a Special Account, which is used for little extras for our residents."

"What happened this year?" Brooke spoke so softly,

it would have been easy to miss the change in intonation.

Jennie didn't. "Your paper has already covered that."

"But nobody's ever pinned down the connection between the transfer and the murder of Robert Payton."

The cards were on the table now. There was no need for cat and mouse. Jennie answered accordingly. "You have to talk to the police about that. Lieutenant Masoski is the officer in charge of the investigation."

"But you're the one who discovered the body . . . and you helped count the Gala money."

Darn you, Alice. I'm the last person who should be talking to the press right now.

Brooke persisted. "Aren't you?"

"I helped count the money. Then I gave it to someone from the bank. After that, I was out of the loop."

"Isn't it true that you gave it to Robert Payton, and he ended up dead? Murdered?"

Jennie knew her only hope was to steer the interview in a new direction. But first she needed to put herself in the driver's seat. She decided a direct approach would be best. "Look, I'm not going to talk about the crimes or the investigations of them. You said you wanted to do a feature on our Fourth of July celebration. I'll tell you anything I know about that."

"You discovered the body."

"That's already been covered in your paper. There's no need for me to add more."

"You were at the bank earlier today, questioning bank employees."

"I wasn't questioning the employees. I had a lunch date with one of them."

"My source said—"

"Your 'source'? Who's that?"

Brooke sat quietly biting her lip, shaking her head. "You know I can't tell you."

"And I can't talk to you about anything except our celebration. It may not be as hot as a crime investigation, but there's a story there—one people will actually enjoy reading. Talk to some of our residents. They'll tell you what Independence Day means to them."

There was a flicker in Brooke's eyes.

Jennie noted it but wasn't deceived into thinking she'd diverted the reporter. *She thinks she can pump them and they won't know what she's doing.* That didn't bother Jennie. She had confidence in her residents. "Come on. This time of day the lounge'll be full of people watching *Oprah.* I'll introduce you around." Without waiting for an answer, Jennie bounced out of her chair and headed for the hall.

Brooke followed, pad and pen in hand, stiletto heels clicking.

As predicted, the lounge was full. Nobody had trouble transferring their interest from the TV when Jennie explained who Brooke was and what she wanted.

The residents, especially the older men, competed for air time, telling Brooke what a great country we live in and what a wonderful tradition the celebration of our independence is.

Jennie watched Brooke's expression go from mildly interested to polite but bored, and, finally, to overwhelmed. Time for a rescue mission. "Thanks, guys. I think she has enough for her article." She turned to Brooke. "Right?"

"Yes." The simple word conveyed immeasurable gratitude.

Jennie needed to get the reporter out of there, but the veterans didn't look anywhere near ready to stop with their stories.

"Maybe I should show her where we stage the fireworks." She turned to Brooke. "Would you like that?"

"Sure."

"Let's go. I have to pick up a key."

Chapter Sixteen

Jennie glanced into Nate's room as they passed.

The old actor was sitting on his bed, shoulders slumped, hands between his knees, staring into space.

She couldn't leave him like that. She took Brooke's elbow and guided her to Nate's doorway. "Want to meet one of the best actors who ever trod the boards?" The words were directed to Brooke but were loud enough for Nate to hear.

His posture changed. His face assumed a theatrical frown. "What's this *'one* of the best' business?"

"Okay, *the* best," Jennie said. She eased Brooke into the room.

Nate rose, now all smiles. "Pleased to meet you. I'm Nathaniel Pynchon." He executed an exaggerated bow and, with a sweep of his arm, directed Brooke's attention to the lineup of framed clippings and playbills that covered his walls.

She didn't look impressed.

Jennie watched Nate take this in and wanted to give the reporter a good, swift kick. She said to Nate, "Things are kind of dull in the lounge. Maybe you can drum up a card game. Liven things up."

"Who wants to play cards with a bunch of old coots?" He reached out to straighten a frame holding a yellowed clipping.

The bid for attention seemed to sail over Brooke's head.

Jennie reflected on her fate: stuck between a grumpy old actor and a bored young reporter. Well, maybe she could kill two birds with one stone. The challenge of a tough conquest might snap Nate out his funk. And, once that happened, Nate just might charm Brooke into writing a glowing account about Riverview. And maybe Leda would read it over her breakfast tomorrow morning and be so pleased, she'd coax Preston into thawing the trust enough to pay Jennie's salary. *And maybe I'll win a million dollars tonight at the dog track.* Oh, well, at the very least, she could amuse Nate and distract Brooke for half an hour or so.

She took his arm. "Want to come out to the island with us?"

"Island?" Brook dropped her notebook and stooped to pick it up.

Nate clarified. "We shoot the fireworks off from an island just out from our shoreline." On his way to the hall, he paused to check his reflection in the mirrored closet door. After a moment's study, he opened the closet and selected a yachting cap, which he perched over his silvery mane at a jaunty angle. Another consultation with the mirror, a minute adjustment, and he sauntered forth. "Coming, mateys?"

Jennie followed.

Brooke, seemingly rooted to the tiles, did not. "I should be getting back."

"Without your story?" Jennie coaxed. "Come on, this is your chance to cover Riverview Manor from an angle no one has."

Brooke neither agreed nor disagreed. She remained quiet as she followed Jennie and Nate through the halls, out the door, and across River Road.

Jennie noted the silence but was confident that Brooke would be won over when they reached the island—to Jennie, a magical place she never tired of exploring. The thought of it quickened her steps and pushed everyday problems to the back of her mind. She skipped down the wooden stairs that led from the bike path to the small boathouse at the river's edge. When she reached the bottom, she looked up to check on Nate. His progress was slow, his concentration intense. She resisted the urge to go back and help but watched closely, ready to dash up at the slightest misstep.

"Knees aren't what they used to be," he said when he joined her on the level surface.

The admission saddened her. There were few things Nate hated as much as being reminded he was eighty-four years old.

"Worth it, though, isn't it?" He pointed to the brown water coursing by.

"Oh, yes." Jennie breathed deeply and took a minute to watch the river, as alive as any sentient creature. It had been a dry spring and summer, so the Mississippi rested low, exposing eight feet of gravel between the dock and the grass.

Jennie slipped off her sandals and set them on the bottom step, then searched for the largest, levelest stones and used them to hopscotch her way across the rocky expanse. She unlocked the chain that secured the fourteen-foot runabout to the dock and tossed the keys onto the seat of the boat.

Nate was right behind her, ready to climb aboard. She steadied him as he stepped in. As usual, he didn't accept help without a grumble. "No need to treat me like I'm made of eggs."

"I know. Humor me, though. If I don't help you guys, I'm out of a job, and I need the money."

Jennie was so intent on assuaging Nate's ego, she didn't realize Brook hadn't followed them until she looked up and saw her peering down from the top of the stairs.

"Come on!" Jennie called.

"I'd rather not."

"Why?"

"No reason." Brooke hesitated, then held up one foot, displaying a high-heeled, backless slide. Her grin was apologetic. "I didn't plan on a river outing when I got dressed this morning."

"Gotcha," Jennie said. "Neither did I." She spread her hands, indicating her own attire, the sundress she'd worn to her lunch date at the bank. She held up one bare foot and wiggled her toes. "Take your shoes off. You'll be fine."

"I saw how you hopped over the rocks. I don't think I can do that."

"Feet too tender?"

Brooke bobbed her head and grimaced.

Jennie looked around until she saw a couple of boards the river had washed up. Their surfaces were silvery gray, polished smooth by the water. Jennie retrieved them and formed a walkway across the gravel to the dock. She looked up at Brooke and spread her arms in a wide flourish. "Here. A path fit for a princess."

Brooke still looked doubtful.

Nate mumbled, "If I can do it, she can."

Jennie shot him a chastising look and looked up to Brooke. "Nobody's ever written about this. You'd be the first."

"I can't swim."

How can anybody live in a river town and not swim? Jennie tried to reassure her. "The boat's small, but it's sturdy. Besides, we have life jackets. Even one of these things." She held up a Styrofoam doughnut.

Brooke's posture was rigid as she looked down toward the river. Finally, she slipped off her shoes and started down the steps.

When she reached the boat and climbed in, Jennie handed her a bright orange life jacket.

Brooke wrinkled her nose and held the item at arm's length. "Not my best color."

At least she has a sense of humor. Jennie felt a reluctant sympathy toward the reporter. "You don't have to wear it," she said. "It's not even a hundred yards out to the island. I doubt we'll sink in that distance." What Jennie did not point out was that this narrow stretch was one of the most treacherous parts of the river, where the water, diverted by the island, ran swiftly and cut a deep channel.

Brooke looked across to the island, then down into the swirling, muddy water before she slipped the jacket over her head and pulled the straps tight, an incongruous accessory to her pearls and stylish dress.

Jennie guided the boat to a sandy area of the island's shoreline, hiked up her skirt, and hopped out. She pulled on the rope, easing the craft farther in, then secured it to a tree.

Nate clambered out, with Brooke right behind him. She removed the life jacket and tossed it into the boat.

Jennie said, "What? You don't want to make a fashion statement?"

Brooke ignored the teasing remark. "What do you do out here, anyway?"

Jennie pointed to a level expanse at the northern tip of the island, about ten yards from where they stood. "We shoot off the fireworks from there. Since it's in the middle of the river, there's no danger of fire." She gestured across the river and up the hill with Riverview hugging its crest. "We sit up there on the lawn and watch the show. It's a great vantage point. Even with cars parked all along River Road, the slope is enough that we can see over the cars."

"Who sets off the fireworks? You?"

"Oh, no. We have professionals come out. That's one of the extra perks our Gala money pays for."

"Speaking of the Gala . . ."

Jennie gave herself a mental kick and held up a hand to silence Brooke. "If you're going to ask about the transfer or the murder, don't. I already told you I can't discuss them."

"Then there's no point in our being here." Brooke flounced away in the direction of the boat.

"No point?" Jennie couldn't help it. She really didn't understand this woman. "Look around you." She threw her arms wide, sweeping them in an arc that encompassed the river, a glossy brown with hints of gold where a slight breeze sent ripples over its surface, and the island itself, the myriad colors of the rocks, the tall maples that grew in its center. A giant swallowtail lit on a stone and fluttered bright wings. Jennie pointed it out to Brooke. "Isn't that worth a story? And that?" She pointed upward to a swirl of clouds floating in a sky the color of a robin's egg.

Brooke sighed heavily.

Nate said, "I don't think the lady's a nature lover, Jennie. That's not the story she wants."

Brooke looked at him. "Thank you very much." The words were heavy with sarcasm. She turned to Jennie. "Okay, I agree. It's pretty, but . . ." She shrugged. "As far as I'm concerned, we may as well go back." She returned to the boat, climbed in, and stood with her back to the others, staring ahead, clutching the life jacket in front of her.

Jennie helped Nate into the boat. This time he didn't protest. He took a seat in the stern and gazed thoughtfully at Brooke, who moved away from him but continued to stand.

Jennie muttered under her breath the whole time she was untying the boat and pushing it back into the river. "Why did I think this was a good idea?" She vowed to apologize and at least not send Brooke off with a completely negative opinion of Riverview. She got into the boat, started it, and steered back toward the shore. She remained standing, loving the feel of the breeze pushing up over the windshield and ruffling her hair. Once they were under way, she half turned so she could see Brooke and still keep one eye on the river.

Jennie said. "I thought you'd like to see Riverview Manor from a different perspective."

Brooke, who stood beside Jennie, the life jacket clasped to her chest with both hands, snapped back, "I don't like being stonewalled."

Jennie kept her voice level. "When you called, you said you wanted to do a feature about our Fourth of July celebration. That's what I was trying to tell you about."

Brooke stepped closer. "Yes, but—"

The boat lurched, almost flipping over.

Jennie gripped the wheel and scanned the river. No, she hadn't steered into a whirlpool; there was no sign of a submerged log. The boat was now rocking wildly. She looked toward the back. Nate was on his feet, moving forward, both arms outstretched. The scene unfolded in slow motion.

"No! Don't!" Jennie's words merged with Brooke's scream, which was followed by a huge splash and Nate's mischievous laugh.

Brooke was in the water, spewing mouthfuls of the Big Muddy. Released from her flailing arms, the life jacket headed for the Gulf of Mexico. Dazed, Jennie watched the perfectly coiffed head go under while the safety gear bobbed irretrievably away, a tiny orange blemish on Old Man River's imperturbable surface.

She can't swim!

Jennie cut the motor and dived. Her fingertips sliced the surface. Liquid like warm milk flowed over her arms, her face, her shoulders. A pocket of cold water, lurking just below the surface, slapped her in the face. She gasped and inhaled, choking on a mouthful of the famously gritty river. She arched her body upward and emerged, wheezing and coughing. *Where's Brooke?* She ignored the stinging in her eyes, forced them to remain open, and finally spotted the reporter downstream. "Kick your feet!" Jennie yelled. Three strong strokes, aided by the current, put Jennie alongside the panic-stricken girl. She treaded water, avoiding the thrashing arms, and managed to get an elbow under Brooke's chin. "I've got you."

Brooke grabbed Jennie's arms with both hands, almost pulling her under.

The gauzy sundress fabric wrapped around Jennie's legs like a thin sheet of lead. *I can't do this.* She kept her hold on Brooke and yelled into her ear. "Stop fighting!" *I have to.* She forced her legs to continue pumping and spoke again, calmer this time. "We're okay." *Please, please, God, make it true.* She looked for the boat. It was about ten yards upstream. Nate was standing in the back, with a life preserver in his hands. Even from where she was, Jennie read the fear in his face. She yelled, "Throw it!"

The Styrofoam doughnut landed just out from the boat, then bobbed and danced until the current caught it. Jennie kicked in place and waited for it to reach them. She snagged it and placed one of Brooke's hands around it. "Hold on to this. I won't let you go."

Brooke snatched the life preserver with a force that took both her and Jennie under.

"Relax," Jennie said when they surfaced. "And hold on to that doughnut."

Brooke nodded a frantic concurrence.

The current was taking the boat and the two women downstream at the same pace.

"All we have to do is paddle a few feet and we'll be back to the boat." Jennie spoke with more confidence than she felt, knowing both their lives depended on her ability to control Brooke's panic. When they were within touching distance of the boat, she said, "I'm going to let you go. Keep one hand on the preserver and grab the side of the boat with the other." She felt the tension in Brooke's body. "You can do it. Just reach up with this hand." She guided Brooke's free hand up until it rested on the boat's side. "Good girl. A few minutes more and we'll be back on dry land."

Brooke nodded. Mascara streaked her cheeks, and her hair hung in strings around her face.

Jennie looked up at Nate, standing over them. "There's a ladder under the bow. Get it and hang it over the side."

He extracted the ladder from a coil of rope, unfolded it, and hung it on the boat.

"You first," Jennie said.

When Brooke tried to climb the ladder, the boat tipped and knocked her backward.

Jennie grabbed her and placed her hand on a rung of the ladder. "Move to the other side," she yelled at Nate. "We need ballast over there."

He did as he was told.

Brooke managed to scramble up the ladder to safety and collapsed into the seat.

When Jennie got back into the boat, Brooke was shivering despite the sun beating down and a temperature that was still over the ninety-degree mark. Jennie tried to reassure her. "Just hold on a couple more minutes." The ride back was quiet except for the thrumming of the motor. Nate and Brooke sat in the back together, shoulders almost touching, neither looking at the other.

Chapter Seventeen

Riverview Manor occupied the crest of a hill that rose above the Mississippi's eastern bank, so it took the full blaze of the late-afternoon sun. Jennie, Nate, and Brooke trudged up the hill to the accompaniment of a million buzzing insects. Human conversation was nil.

Nate whistled. *Row, row, row your boat.* When he reached *Life is but a dream,* he caught Jennie's eye with a wicked grin. She glared at him, giving new meaning to the cliché about looks that could kill.

Brooke ignored them and stalked ahead.

Jennie alternated between wondering what Brooke's next column would say and trying not to think about it.

Riverview's windows reflected a dazzle of light, rendering the glass opaque. The wicker chairs that graced the veranda were empty. The only signs of life were three squirrels chasing one another around the columns. There was no doubt in Jennie's mind, however, that behind those black panes, eyes were watching, heads were bobbing, tongues were wagging, and, most of all, imaginations were working overtime.

The front door jerked open with a ferocity that sent the squirrels scrambling. Alice Telford marched out. "What on earth?"

Jennie looked past Alice and saw faces peering over the woman's shoulder, bodies edging closer. Without exception, the faces echoed Alice's amazed query. Jennie glanced at Brooke, who, when last seen by any of these people, had been the epitome of chic sophistication. Now she possessed the elegance of a river rat. Jennie doubted the smart linen dress would ever be restored to its original icy blue. Even the sassy city-girl shoes showed signs of her ordeal. They hadn't been in the river, but during the trek up the hill, one heel had snapped.

The hem of Jennie's dress clung to her legs, reminding her that she must look at least as bad.

"Well?" Alice demanded.

Jennie was still searching for a way to explain when Nate stepped forward in military style. "We had a little accident." In sharp contrast to his companions, he was as dapper as ever. His pale tan trousers retained their knife-like crease. The yachting cap was perched at the same rakish angle. His back was ramrod straight, and his eyes sparkled. If he felt remorse for the debacle he'd caused, he hid it well.

Alice dismissed him with a cursory glance and focused on Jennie. Her slitted eyes and pursed lips demanded an explanation.

"Our Jennie saved this young woman's life." Nate paused to make eye contact with each member of his audience, held his hand over his heart, and seemed to choke up. "It was a sight to make us all proud."

Brooke, the young woman in question, darted a viper look in Nate's direction and limped into the building, presumably heading for her car in the rear parking lot. The crowd parted before her like a zipper opening.

Alice ran after her. "Is there anything I can do?"

No response.

Alice tried again. "Maybe a nice cup of tea?"

Brooke whirled. "Only if you put a slug of Jack Daniels in it."

Alice blinked. She looked as if she could use a shot herself.

A maintenance worker pushing a trash cart through the hall was obviously enjoying the spectacle. He made a valiant but unsuccessful effort to control his mirth when Brooke stopped inches from where he stood.

She glared at him, then stooped to remove her ruined shoes, which she dropped, one by one, into the cart, and continued her trek through the corridor without another word. Her bare feet slapping the tile floor spoke volumes.

Alice turned to Jennie, eyebrows raised.

Jennie had never seen Alice angry before. She almost wished Leda were back.

The residents, always Jennie's defenders, formed a phalanx around her.

Jennie looked Alice in the eye and held up one hand. "Half an hour to clean up?"

"Fifteen minutes." Alice stalked off toward the Executive Director's office.

Fine time for her to develop a backbone. Jennie was beginning to think that maybe Alice *could* fill Leda's shoes. Jennie's first stop was the Activities Room. She rooted in the supply closet until she found a pair of faded jeans and a paint-spattered T-shirt, then headed for the showers.

Georgie intercepted her halfway there. "Here," she said, and she pressed a bar of soap into Jennie's hand.

Jennie put the soap to her nose and recognized the scent—Chanel No. 5. "This is from your granddaughter. I can't—"

"Sure, you can," Georgie said. "Megan sends these little presents for my pleasure. And nothing would give me more pleasure than to give you a little splurge right now. I think you could use it."

When Jennie opened her mouth to thank her, the feisty ninety-year-old put a finger to her lips. "Shh," she said. "I have my reputation to think of."

Twenty minutes later, Jennie presented herself to Alice, scruffily-dressed but showered and sweet-smelling. Since Riverview had rules against employees traipsing through the halls barefoot, she'd put her wet sandals back on. The soles squished with each step.

Alice looked her up and down without comment.

Jennie felt she had to explain. "These were the only dry clothes I could find." She held the shirtfront, stiff with amber-colored paint, away from her body. "I wore this when I helped Doreen redecorate her room."

Alice leaned back and picked up a pencil. "You don't have to remind me of all the extra things you do for our residents."

"That's not—"

Alice cut her off, waving the pencil like a baton. "I

know—everybody knows—that you always put forth a thousand percent . . . but . . ." Alice's voice drifted, and she scratched her head with the pencil. "Trouble seems to find you. You know how important it is that we put our best foot forward for the press. Especially now."

Following the example of her father, an avid sports fan, Jennie decided a strong offense was her best defense. She stood straight and lifted her chin. "I didn't want to talk to that reporter. It was your job, and you foisted it off on me." She watched Alice recoil and pressed on. "You were right when you suspected she wanted to talk about the stolen funds and the murder. Two minutes after you left she started in, asking questions I couldn't answer. If you'd been there, you could have said you didn't know anything."

"Why couldn't you say that?"

"She knew I'd helped Rob Payton count the money and that I was the one who found his body. I was the last person who should have been in that position."

Alice's newfound bravado was ebbing fast. She slumped back in her chair. "You're right. I should have talked to her myself." The old Alice was back, lovable but ineffectual.

On the one hand, Jennie was relieved; on the other, she felt as if she'd just kicked a puppy. She tried to make amends. "It doesn't matter. Assigning blame won't help anyone. The important thing is to figure out how to make it right."

Alice nodded, then tilted her head and almost smiled. "First, tell me what happened."

Jennie stalled, considering what to say. She curled her toes and felt the dampness squish between them. For some reason not even she understood, she wanted to protect Nate, even if it was only from himself. "Brooke fell overboard."

"Were you going too fast?" Alice, though she was unmarried and had no children, looked every inch a disapproving mother.

"No, I wasn't going fast at all. Hardly moving, in fact. But Brooke was standing up in the boat, next to me. We were talking. Nate was sitting in the back. Next thing I knew, she was in the river. To tell the truth, it's kind of a blur. I'm not sure how it happened." Jennie let it go at that. She hadn't actually lied. Told only half-truths, perhaps, but it was a story she thought she could live with. It crossed her mind that Nate might be regaling other residents with a different version, one that cast him in the role of heroic figure. One thing in her favor—most people believed only about a tenth of what Nate said.

Alice leaned forward. "That's it?"

"Pretty much."

"Nate said you saved Brooke's life. Is that true?"

"Kinda. She was holding on to a life jacket when she went overboard, and somehow . . . I guess the impact when she hit the water . . . she let the jacket go, and it floated away. She started screaming because she couldn't swim. I jumped in, and, when I got hold of her, Nate threw the life preserver. Between the two of us, we got her back into the boat."

"So, you actually did save her life. Once she calms down, she should be grateful. She'll have every reason to write something positive about Riverview Manor. She might even find the whole episode humorous."

"That's possible." Jennie tried not to let her doubt

show. She changed the subject. "Enough of that. What do we do now?"

Alice tented her fingers and moved on to damage control. "I think it would be appropriate for you to give her a call. Make sure she's recovered. See if you can guide the direction of her article."

"I don't think that's a good idea. If I try to tell her what to say . . ."

"Maybe you're right. But call her. Let her know you're concerned."

How am I gonna get out of this? "I don't have her number. She didn't leave a card or anything."

"Call the paper. Get the number from them." Alice was in her element now. She loved administrative detail. "At least you can leave a message." She favored Jennie with her sweetest smile. "I'll leave it to your discretion." She gathered the papers on her desk, tapped them on the polished surface until their edges were precisely aligned, and placed them in a folder. She glanced at her watch. "Goodness, it's going on five. I have to leave." Another sugary smile. "Do me a favor. Stick around. Have dinner with the residents. This whole series of events is bound to upset them. They respond to you. You'll be able to put them at ease." Another smile, this time one of dismissal. As Jennie turned to leave, Alice said, "It is a delicate situation, but I'm confident you're up to it."

Delicate? Yes, at the very least, that. Jennie left the office, knowing the situation, however it unfolded, was hers to deal with.

Chapter Eighteen

Jennie's sandals left a damp trail from the Executive Director's office to the dining room. She paused in the doorway, conscious of the ripped jeans and ratty T-shirt. Most residents were old-school and dressed, if not formally, at least neatly, for dinner. She scanned the room and headed for the staff table in a corner, hoping to eat alone. She needed to organize her thoughts and formulate a plan for dealing with the situation so aptly described by Alice as *delicate*.

It was not to be.

Nate spotted her, rose, and began to applaud.

Others joined in, and Jennie found herself the embarrassed recipient of a standing ovation. Tears pricked the corners of her eyes. She knew she should say something but didn't dare, afraid the dam holding back the tears would break. She stood, gripped the table edge for support, and nodded.

The residents seemed to understand. All except Nate

sat back down. Nate ambled over, ignoring the tacit agreement that staff, when seated at their special table in the corner, needed a little downtime. He pulled out a chair at Jennie's right elbow and leaned in to whisper, "Nothing to worry about. I've managed to spin today's events in our favor."

Jennie resisted the temptation to bury her face in her hands and give way to the torrent of emotions warring within. Instead, she smiled at Nate and, exercising every ounce of patience she possessed, said, "We need to talk, but not now."

He sat back and studied her. His blue eyes projected understanding worthy of an archangel.

Jennie held up one hand before he could say anything. "Right now, I'm going to have a cup of tea and something to eat. And I really need some time to myself."

Nate stiffened his spine.

She recognized the posture and knew he was preparing a speech, probably something grandiose from his days in the theater. She wasn't in the mood. "I mean it, Nate. You've gone too far this time."

"So I'm not even allowed to explain? Don't you want to hear why I did what I did?"

"Not until after I've eaten."

Jennie was aware, and she was certain Nate was, that everyone in the room was watching them.

He stood, clamped a hand on her shoulder, and spoke loudly enough for everyone to hear. "We'll talk later, dear." He kissed her on the cheek, then, smiling and nodding for the benefit of his audience, glided back to his table, head held high.

From the corner of her eye, Jennie saw him signal to

the tea ladies to leave her alone. Not that they, or anyone else, needed a reminder. Everyone except Nate respected the unwritten rules that made it possible for a large number of people to live and work in close proximity on a daily basis.

Jennie knew that Nate's arrogance was camouflage for a fragile though oversized ego, and most of the time she was happy to serve as a buffer between his fantasy world and mundane reality. Just now, she'd hurt his feelings. Another problem to be dealt with. *Later.* At the moment she was exhausted and too frazzled to think about it. She picked at the chicken and rice casserole, didn't bother with the overcooked broccoli, and pushed her plate aside and concentrated on the tea, a pleasant herbal blend with a hint of lemon.

Other diners finished and started wandering from the room. Jennie stood and tapped a fork against her glass for attention. "How about some games in the Activities Room?" she said, forcing cheer into her voice.

Doreen, who was near the door, swiveled her wheelchair and squinted at Jennie. "You sure you feel up to it?"

"It's been a full day," Jennie admitted, "but I could use a little diversion. I'll go set up the room as soon as I finish eating."

A voice from near the windows boomed, "Maybe you can fill us in on what's going on around here."

"I think that's in order," Jennie said, not sure what she'd say about the afternoon's disaster but aware that giving no explanation would start the rumor mill whirling.

She snagged an aide on her way to the Activities Room and asked him to help her move some tables and chairs. With his help, she set up several different areas, close enough to encourage conversation but with enough space between them that residents could play separate games without distracting one another. That done, she went to a tall bank of cabinets and pulled out an assortment of games. She put Balderdash on a round table set up for six. She lay Trivial Pursuit at one end of a long, narrow table, knowing that a dozen or so residents would arrange themselves into two teams and settle in for a cutthroat game. Tribond was set up in similar fashion and, of course, the well-worn Monopoly board came out. Checkers and dominoes were placed in a prominent spot on her desk.

Residents drifted in, some alone, some in pairs or small groups, and found seats at whatever table featured their favorite game. They scraped their chairs into position and shuffled boxes and game boards, but no one started to play.

Jennie waited for the inquisition to begin.

Georgie took the lead. "Well, what happened?"

No need to ask what she meant.

"I'm not sure," Jennie said, careful to stick to the story she'd told Alice. "It all happened so fast. One minute Brooke was standing in the boat, talking to me. The next she went sailing overboard. I didn't actually see her trip or anything, but I guess she must have." It was only a small lie, one Jennie hoped was at least reasonably close to whatever story Nate had told. She trusted he'd had the sense not to confess to knocking Brooke in, though he might have. It would definitely put him in the spotlight, his favorite location.

"That's it?" Georgie demanded.

Someone else spoke up. "She seemed pretty mad."

"Maybe she was more embarrassed," Jennie suggested. After that, questions and comments flew so fast and furious, Jennie couldn't keep up with who said what.

"What were you doing out there on the river anyway?"

"Did the boat capsize?"

"How come Nate didn't get wet?"

"Who was that woman? I never saw her around here before."

"Did you really save her life?"

Jennie didn't have to say a word. Someone else always came up with an answer until everyone had been filled in on what had happened. Surprisingly, the version they ended up with was not too far from the truth—except no one hinted that Nate had knocked Brooke into the river. Somehow he'd left out that not-so-minor detail. In fact, there was little mention of Nate. And no one seemed to care what Jennie had to say. They were happy shaping the afternoon into their own folk tale.

Jennie excused herself and went to Nate's room. She found him reading the theater section of last Sunday's *New York Times*. She knocked and, when he looked up, entered the room. She closed the door behind her and didn't bother with niceties. "Why did you do it?"

"I think that's obvious."

"Not to me. To me, it just seems mean. Especially when you knew she couldn't swim."

"I forgot about that." He gazed into her eyes, daring her to call him a liar.

She didn't. Jennie would never speak like that to a resident, but she didn't try to mask what she thought. "Even so. Why'd you do it? The Mississippi is a dangerous river, even for a strong swimmer. It could have been a tragedy."

He pouted. "She was threatening my home."

"I assume you mean Riverview?" When he nodded, she added, "How was she threatening Riverview?"

"By the questions she was asking. I saw where she was headed. She had every intention of writing a sensational exposé about what a hotbed of crime we have here." Nate's posture grew more indignant with each word. By the time he finished, he had cast himself in the dual role of injured party and Riverview's savior.

Nice try, Jennie thought, but she wasn't about to let him get away with it. "You gave her a reason to write something twice as nasty. Like maybe we took her out in a boat and tried to drown her."

"Why? Because she's so clumsy, she fell overboard?"

"Stop it! We both know she didn't 'fall' overboard."

He looked down, then up, peering at her through his eyelashes, his you-know-you-love-me expression. "Did you tell Alice that?"

She didn't answer, but it was clear he knew she hadn't. He persisted. "Did you?"

"No, I—"

A knock on the door interrupted.

"Who is it?" Nate asked.

Karen, the night receptionist, opened the door partway and stuck her head in, grinning. She looked at Jennie. "You have a visitor," she said. "A man. Fine-lookin' man."

Ohmigod. Karl!

"Where is he?" Jennie deserted Nate and joined Karen in the hall.

"Waiting in the lounge. I'd have taken him to the Activities Room, but it's full of residents." She affected a salacious look. "I thought you might want a little privacy."

"Does he seem angry?"

"Not so's I could tell. Why? Does he have a reason to be?"

"He might think so."

They reached the lounge and found Karl Erickson perched on a love seat, studying the hulking object draped with black cloth. When he saw Jennie, he tilted his head and asked, "What's that?"

"A birdcage."

"Must be a big bird."

"A lot of small birds," Jennie explained. "You know how some businesses fill their offices with plants and pay a service to come in and take care of them? Well, we have birds."

"Do you have a service to take care of them?"

"Yes. And between their visits, I feed the birds, make sure they have water. The residents love them."

He reached for the cloth. "May I look?"

Jennie stilled his hand. "We try not to disturb them after dark. Especially now. Some little ones just hatched."

He looked at Jennie's hand on his wrist and cupped his over it. "You stood me up."

"I'm sorry." Aware that Karen was watching, Jennie removed her hand, didn't know what to do with it, then finally stuck it into her pocket.

Karl followed the action with his eyes, seeming to take in her attire for the first time. "Nice ensemble."

"I took an unexpected dip this afternoon." She laughed to cover her embarrassment.

"Somebody push you into the exercise pool?"

"Think bigger. This was Old Man River himself. That's why I for—"

He didn't let her finish. "Don't say you forgot. That's hard on a guy's ego."

"If you knew the day I've had, you'd understand."

"So, tell me about it. Have you eaten?"

"Yes." She admitted it with regret. It felt good to be with someone who didn't have a problem for her to solve.

"Well, I haven't. Can I at least talk you into a cup of coffee to keep me company?" His face broke into that crooked smile again. "Don't forget, I'm on your list. You still have to question me."

She laughed. "Okay. I had dinner here, and . . ." She lowered her voice to a stage whisper. "Frankly, it was pretty bad. Let's go across the alley to Lilly's Place, and I'll have dessert."

He looked surprised. "Lilly's? I thought they closed early."

"They do. Officially. But Riverview staff can go in through the back, and Lilly always finds something for us."

"Is that legal?"

Jennie shrugged. "I guess. There's usually at least one cop in there having coffee."

He looked a little nervous, but he said, "Let's go."

"I have something to check on first. I got the residents started on a game night, then deserted them."

Karl followed her to the Activities Room and stood by her side while she told the residents she was leaving, but they should go on playing. When she spoke, the click of game pieces and the buzz of conversation stopped while everyone in the room, especially the tea ladies, gave Karl more than a casual once-over. Georgie, in particular, looked ready to pounce. Thank God Nate wasn't there.

Jennie said her good-byes and made a quick exit—not that she had any illusions that that would spare her an explanation. She knew Georgie would be lying in wait the next morning.

Chapter Nineteen

Jennie had been right. Two cops were hunched over a table, enjoying coffee and Lilly's famous pecan pie. Jasmine, Lilly's rebellious sixteen-year-old daughter, hovered, flirting with the younger one. When Jennie entered, Jasmine gave her a quick glance, then did an extended double take when she saw Karl. She sauntered over. "Hi, Mrs. Conners," she purred. "You come in for some of Mom's pie?"

"Any left?" Jennie hid her amusement. Jasmine usually didn't have the time of day for her. Karen had been right. Karl was a fine-looking man.

Lilly came in from the kitchen. When she saw Jennie, she called across the room, "Haven't seen you for a few days, but I've been reading about you in the papers. Can't stay out of trouble, can you? You're worse than my girls."

Karl strode over to her and offered his hand. "You must be Lilly. I'm Karl. Glad to meet you. Hear you've got the best pecan pie in Memphis."

"I won't argue with that. Bad for business." When he turned his back, Lilly flashed a thumbs-up sign.

Jennie couldn't suppress a smile.

Karl noticed and said, "You ladies laughing at me?" Instead of answering him, Jennie said to Lilly, "Karl hasn't had dinner. Anything left in the kitchen?"

"I can always grill some veggies for a sandwich."

Karl didn't look enthusiastic.

Jennie came to her friend's defense. "You've obviously never tasted one of Lilly's veggie sandwiches. Believe me, you're in for a treat. You may never order steak again." Without waiting for him to answer, she said to Lilly, "We'd appreciate it. I'll have some dessert. Any pie left?"

"Last time I checked, there was one piece. Charly had her eye on it, though, so I'm not making promises."

With that, Lilly's youngest daughter, a nine-year-old tomboy, stuck her head out of the kitchen. "Hi, Mrs. Conners," she said. "I thought I heard your voice. You heard from Tommy?"

"They called yesterday. They're on a trail ride somewhere in Arizona."

"When's he's coming home?"

"Nine more days." It seemed like forever.

Lilly interrupted. "Charly, is that piece of pie still there?"

The little girl hesitated. "Sorta."

"Sorta?"

Charly looked at the floor, then back at her mother. "I ate half of it."

Lilly rolled her eyes at Jennie. "You feel like half a piece of pie?"

Jennie glanced from mother to daughter. "That's more than enough. Maybe Charly and I can split it."

Charly bobbed her head and grinned.

Lilly gave her daughter's ponytail a playful tug. "I'll go work on that sandwich."

Jennie led Karl to a round table in a corner of the dining room.

When they were seated, he said, "Seem like nice folks."

"The best."

He looked around the spacious room, then inclined his head toward the bright Polynesian quilts decorating the white walls. "She's from Hawaii, right? Married into an old Memphis family?"

Jennie nodded.

Jasmine waltzed out with coffee. "Mom said to tell you your food'll be ready in a couple of minutes."

"Thanks," Jennie said.

Karl watched her leave, then asked, "Wasn't there some trouble here a little while back?"

"Yes, but it didn't have anything to do with Lilly or her family. It was just bad luck they were involved."

He regarded her seriously. "You're very loyal to your friends, aren't you?"

She felt her cheeks flush and couldn't have said why. "I guess so."

He put his elbows on the table and leaned forward with his face supported by his fists. "That's a nice quality."

Her cheeks were flaming now. She cursed her fair skin.

They smiled at each other. Neither spoke. It was not the comfortable quiet of old friends but a silence that begged to be filled.

Jennie was relieved when Lilly's solid form appeared in the door with Charly by her side.

Karl's eyes widened when Lilly set a plate before him. A colorful medley of squash, onions, and peppers spilled from a long roll. Lilly's secret blend of spices perfumed the air.

Charly carried a dessert plate with a thin sliver of pie. The child grinned at Jennie, then at the two forks crisscrossed near the plate's edge. "You said you wanted to share."

"Yes, I did." Jennie took one bite, savored it, and put her fork down. "Okay, that's all I need. Enough to keep my sweet tooth happy, but not so much that I can't button my jeans." She patted the back of a chair and pushed the plate over. "The rest is yours."

Charly pulled the chair out, then looked at her mother, presumably for permission to join Karl and Jennie at the table.

Lilly didn't notice. Her eyes were on Karl.

He dug into the sandwich. Between mouthfuls he said, "You're right, this is delicious." He took a couple more bites, then flashed that smile again. "It'll never replace steak, though."

Jennie and Lilly's eyes met. Lilly signaled approval, and Jennie pushed back her doubts about Karl.

Lilly put her hand on her daughter's shoulder. "Come on, baby, you can finish that pie in the kitchen, then help me clean up."

When they were gone, the silence came back, this time less obvious because Karl was eating.

Jennie toyed with her coffee, turning the cup around

in the saucer. She said, "If you've never been here before, you must be fairly new to Memphis."

"Two years," Karl said, stringing out his words in a tantalizingly slow drawl. "So, the questioning begins."

Jennie took advantage of the opening. "Well, I wouldn't want to be accused of bringing you here under false pretenses. Where're you from? Obviously somewhere in the South."

"Tuscaloosa, Alabama." He swallowed his last bite and pushed the plate to the center of the table, then held up one hand, palm out. "Why don't I just tell you my life story and save you the trouble of asking all those questions?"

"Sure."

"I went to the University of Alabama. Three weeks before graduation I interviewed with Preston Barrons. He offered me a job. That was two years ago, and here I am."

"That's a pretty short life story."

"Well, I'm young yet."

Yes, you are. Very young. "How's Preston to work for? Pretty demanding?"

"Yeah, he's demanding, but that's okay. Anyway, most of my dealings with him were through Rob. Rob was his go-to guy, and I was Rob's assistant."

"What about Rob? How was he to work with?"

"No complaints."

"Were the two of you close?"

"We used to be." Karl's eyes clouded.

"Used to be?"

"We'd go out for drinks after work . . . you know, wait

and start the drive home when the traffic wasn't so hectic." He shrugged. "We didn't do that the last couple of months. I still stopped by his office, but he always made some excuse, had to go straight home."

"He did have a family."

"That's what I told myself at the time, but now I wonder." The silence became too long.

"You think something was going on? Something that led to his murder?"

Karl looked at Jennie and seemed to consider. "Maybe. I've tried to think it through. Looking back, I see a lot of things—little things that didn't seem to mean anything at the time."

"Like what?"

He shrugged again, then hunched forward, his elbows still on the table. "It's hard to say. Nothing to put my finger on." He squinted and seemed to be looking at something only he could see. "For one thing, he spent more time with the kid."

"His daughter, Chloe?"

"No. The Barrons kid. Web."

Jennie remembered Web's statement that Rob had helped him cover mistakes so his father wouldn't find out about them. She didn't mention this, didn't want to put words into Karl's mouth. Instead, she said, "Someone told me the police think Rob transferred the Gala funds out of the Special Account into Web's personal account."

He looked at her sharply. "Who?"

She shrugged off the question. "Doesn't matter. What do you think? Was Rob capable of that?"

"I think anyone is capable of anything. Did he do it? That's another question."

"Well, what do you think? Did he?"

He looked at the ceiling. "I wouldn't go so far as to say he did, but I wouldn't rule it out. I just think . . ." His voice drifted.

"What?"

"Again, it's hard to put a finger on it, but it always seemed a little off to me, the way Rob took Web under his wing."

"Is it possible Web did take the money? That no one was trying to frame him?"

Karl cocked an eyebrow. "If he was anybody else's kid, would there be any question? Money disappears from one account, shows up in another—why not assume the guy who benefited from the transfer is the guy who made it?"

"But it would be a stupid thing to do."

"What if he needed money in a hurry? Thought he could pay it back before anybody found out."

"Sounds like you believe Web made the transfer. Do you think he killed Rob?"

Karl didn't answer.

Jennie kept digging. "Does Web have the computer know-how to move the money?"

"It doesn't take much."

"What about safeguards?"

"He's been around that bank his whole life. He knows a lot more than anyone thinks he does." He spread his hands wide and leaned back so his chair was balanced on two legs. "Hey, I'm not saying he did it."

"Then who?" When he didn't answer right away, she prompted, "You mentioned Rob and Web. Who else has the technical knowledge to transfer the money?"

"Preston himself. He's a very hands-on boss." He half smiled. "I could have done it. I'm the IT guy."

"Did you?"

"Do you really have to ask?"

"Of course I do." She smiled in spite of herself.

"No."

She went on. "Who else? What about Charlotte Ellio?"

"Sure."

"She doesn't seem very technical."

"Because she deleted those files?"

Jennie nodded.

"Don't kid yourself. Charlotte knows a lot more than she lets on. Didn't it occur to you, she didn't want those files found?"

Actually, that hadn't occurred to Jennie, but once Karl mentioned it, it made sense. She said, "I saw you and the other guy—the one who was looking for the files—exchange a look behind Charlotte's back. What was that about?"

"Oh, that's an ongoing joke between Roger and me. Charlotte likes to pretend she doesn't know about computers, but we both think it's an act to get somebody else to do half her work."

"You don't like her, do you?"

"She doesn't like me."

Jennie remembered that that had been her impression. "Why not?"

"She's a dinosaur—doesn't trust me because I make suggestions, try to change things, and she likes to do everything the way it's always been done."

"Is that all?" Jennie was smiling now. "Did you hit on her daughter?"

"Is that what she said?"

"I don't remember her exact words, but that was the gist of it."

"No, I didn't hit on her kid."

"Why does Charlotte think you did?"

"Last Christmas . . . Preston and his wife always have a big do . . . invite everybody who works at the bank, along with their families. . . . Charlotte was there with her daughter. The daughter started flirting with me. I didn't think anything of it. Figured she was just testing her wiles on an older guy. Her mother didn't see it that way. She had a hissy fit." He looked at Jennie. "That's all there was to it. I didn't encourage her."

Jennie remembered sixteen-year-old Jasmine's reaction to Karl when they'd entered the restaurant. He hadn't even seemed to notice. His explanation made sense. As did Charlotte's protection of her daughter. "Okay, enough of that," she said. "Do you think Charlotte stole the money?"

"She has financial problems."

"How do you know?"

"Everybody on the sixth floor knows. We work together. We're tight, like a family."

And now a member of the family had been murdered. Probably by one of its own.

Chapter Twenty

The too-bright headlights turned when Jennie did. She slowed, giving the driver a chance to pass. He slowed, too, then pulled into a 7-Eleven. Good. She had the road to herself now and probably would for the rest of the drive home.

She found herself gripping the steering wheel and flexed her fingers, then leaned back into the seat and rolled her shoulders. It had been quite a day, starting with breakfast with Woody and his mother. Jennie remembered the note Dorothea had shown her when she'd pleaded with Jennie to clear Web. Was Dorothea right? Was someone trying to frame Web for both the funds transfer and the murder? Karl didn't seem to think so. Nor did Charlotte. Of course, Charlotte had been mostly concerned with her lost computer files—files Karl didn't think she wanted found. Now, there was an interesting thought.

What about the text message? *Nobody likes a busybody.*

178

Was it a warning? Should she mention it to Lieutenant Masoski? She waffled on that, first thinking she should, then telling herself there was really nothing threatening about it. She finally decided to keep it to herself and see if more messages appeared. In the meantime, she'd try to match the number with someone's cell phone. Then she'd have something concrete to take to Masoski.

A flash of light stabbed her eyes. She blinked and looked into the mirror. *Darn!* This car's headlights were as bright as the other's had been. Maybe brighter. No, she reasoned, not brighter, the same. *The same? That's paranoid.* She checked the mirror again. If it was the same car, it had been behind her almost since she'd left the restaurant. She glanced at the dashboard clock—10:20. Not late, but on a Tuesday night traffic was usually sparse on the back streets Jennie took to reach her house from Lilly's. With the lights shining in her mirror, she couldn't distinguish the make or even the color of the car behind her.

She turned into her neighborhood. The other vehicle turned, too. She told herself to slow down again to see what happened. Her foot refused to obey her brain. She sped up. The car behind kept the same steady pace. She came to her street, started to turn, then changed her mind and kept going. The other car pulled over to the side just past her street and stopped in front of a dark house.

Somebody's going home. Nothing to do with me. She checked the mirror again. The headlights went off. Jennie watched to see who got out of the other car. No one did. She went straight for two more blocks, then doubled back. The other car was still there, seemingly empty.

There was no one behind her when she turned into her

street. Then, half a block farther, when she pulled into her drive, a set of headlights rounded the corner. Was it the same car? There was no reason to think so, but now she had a raging case of the willies. She grabbed the garage door opener and stabbed at the button. Inside, she made sure the door was completely down before she got out of the car. She kept her eyes on the small windows at the top of the garage door and edged backward toward the house. Her heel struck a hard object. It scraped over the floor and sent a jolt of fear up her spine. She lurched and smashed her elbow into the car. When she looked down, she saw she'd stumbled over a rake. She picked it up and hung it in the tool rack, then placed her hands on the car's hood. She counted to ten, taking slow, deep breaths.

Inside, she locked the door behind her and turned on lights as she passed through the laundry room to the kitchen, then into the family room. As each light went on, its glow spilled over familiar objects, easing her fear. She told herself she was being silly, switched off the lights, and went down the hall to the front bedroom. Silly or not, she couldn't get those headlights out of her mind. She left the room in darkness and watched from the window as the other car drew even with her house. She held her breath as it moved past. Did she imagine it, or was the car going unnaturally slowly? Five minutes later, she was still standing at the window when headlights approached from the opposite direction. The same car? Had it doubled back, checking her house? A magnolia tree partially blocked her view. She strained to see through the branches, squinting, trying to pick out details, pinpoint some distinguishing feature. No luck. The street was dark. All she could see of the car was that it was a light color, maybe white.

The shape was that of a sedan. Jennie couldn't name the make or model.

She went back through the empty house, double-checking the locks on both doors and on every window. She shed her clothes and tumbled into bed, too tired to bother with a shower. Sleep came quickly and brought with it dreams of an unseen menace. Piercing lights that hurt her eyes. Running, going nowhere. Wet, leaden clothing that made every step an effort.

The next morning, still exhausted, Jennie scanned the headlines of the *Commercial Appeal*. A teaser at the top of the front page promised a story by a reporter who'd been fished out of the river. Turn to Section E. *Later.* Jennie finished her English muffin and gulped down some orange juice. She tucked the paper into her tote bag and headed for Riverview, wondering what this day would bring. *Can't be as bad as yesterday.*

"Morning," Annie said when Jennie walked in. "So . . . heard you had a visitor last night."

Jennie's mind immediately jumped to the car that might—or might not—have followed her home. "What do you mean?"

The receptionist's grin stretched from ear to ear. "Heard he's buff."

Jennie realized she meant Karl. "Yeah." She smiled and kept moving. A turn of the corridor and she ran into Woody.

He asked, "Read the paper?"

"Not yet."

"You might want to check it out." He held up a paper,

open to Section E, and folded to reveal the headline: *Is Riverview Manor Trying to Drown Its Sorrows?*

She patted her tote bag and kept walking. "Got a copy. I'll read it later."

He called after her. "I'm trying to be helpful."

She stopped, sorry she'd been so short. Woody Samson was her best friend on the Riverview staff. He was a tease, but she knew he always had her best interests at heart. "How bad is it?" she asked.

"Depends."

"On what?"

"On how much you read between the lines. There's a lot of innuendo about how she fell." He stopped to look at Jennie. "She puts *fell* in quotes every time she uses it. And she uses it a lot." There was a long pause. "I'm guessing that means she was pushed, or at least thinks she was." He arched an eyebrow. "You didn't push her overboard, did you?"

"Of course not."

"Nate?"

"Don't ask." Jennie pointed to the paper. "What else?"

"Well, the gist of it is that every time she tried to ask about the Gala funds, you changed the subject and tried to palm off a story about an innocent little old fireworks display." He lisped the last few words in a high falsetto.

"She came here with the expressed intention of writing about our Fourth of July celebration. Or so she told Alice."

Woody clucked his tongue. "Leda would have seen through that in a heartbeat."

"Alice saw through it, too, but instead of dealing with it, she turned it over to me." Jennie started to walk away.

Woody stopped her with a hand on her arm. "In case you don't get to read the whole article . . . listen to this."

Jennie braced for the worst.

"It's the last sentence." He cleared his throat, then read slowly, enunciating each syllable. " 'Riverview Manor, I will be back.' " Woody looked at Jennie. "Those last four words are in all caps. Thought you might want to know that."

I will be back. Jennie headed for Tess's room with the words singsonging in her head like a bullying playground chant.

The door was open. Tess occupied one of the chairs by her window. She looked as if she'd been waiting. "Come in," she said, and she waved toward the other chair. She held up a folded newspaper and waved it. "Read this yet?"

"Bits and pieces. Enough."

"Want to talk about it?"

Jennie settled into the other chair and stared at the bird feeder attached to the window by a suction cup. "I doubt it'll do any good."

"You're probably right." Tess let the paper drop onto the floor beside her knitting bag. "Enough about Ms. Brooke Newton. I'm sure you'll find a way to deal with her." She leaned forward, her eyes gleaming. "Tell me about that delicious young man you left here with last night."

Jennie laughed. "That's Karl Erickson," she said. "He was Rob Payton's assistant at the bank."

"Oh." Tess settled back in her chair and surveyed Jennie. After a few seconds she asked, "A budding romance, or is he part of your investigation?"

"I told you, I'm not 'investigating' anything."

"So it's a romance?"

"I didn't say that." Was it? Jennie couldn't deny her attraction to Karl, but something kept pulling her back, though she couldn't quite put her finger on what it was. "Can you see him tossing a Frisbee with my boys?" That was as close as she could come.

Tess shrugged and let it go. After a few seconds she said, "I know you don't think it appropriate to involve me in this, and, frankly, I'm disappointed."

"Try to see it from my point of view."

"Oh, I do. You think your responsibility is to protect us residents from worry. That's what Leda's drummed into your head. She's wrong. That's not what we want from you. Or deserve. We deserve respect."

Jennie opened her mouth.

Tess silenced her with a look. "Respect means you treat each of us as an individual." Tess raised her chin.

Jennie said, "It's not that simple."

"Not that complicated either, unless you choose to make it so." Tess paused, seeming to wait for a response. When there was none, she went on, "I notice you include Nate in your plans. He's about as much use as a worn out rubber band. I could actually help." She opened a drawer of the small chest between the chairs and brought out the folder containing the handwriting samples she and Jennie had copied. "I've been studying these."

Jennie couldn't resist. "Oh?"

"First of all, what was the name of that young man again?"

"Karl Erickson."

Tess opened the folder and lifted out bundles of paper, each of which was secured with an oversized paper clip. "Ah, here it is." She glanced at Jennie. "There's no actual writing. Just doodles."

"Can you tell anything from them?"

Tess nodded. "Basically the same rules apply as to handwriting." She removed one bundle and replaced the folder in the drawer. "Sometimes I prefer to work with doodles. There's no temptation to be influenced by the message." She adjusted her glasses, which were sliding down her nose. "That's a personal idiosyncrasy. Not everyone agrees with me."

Jennie leaned closer. "What do you see there?"

"Patience, dear." Tess was obviously enjoying herself. She selected a sheet of paper and spread it on her lap. "Look at this."

Jennie looked at the sketch. There was a straight line with a row of faces above it. Below the line was a row of tiny feet. The faces were well drawn, with a lot of detail, more than the usual doodle.

Tess said, "He must have spent some time on it. My guess is, he was in a meeting and was bored."

"That makes sense. The line could be the table, and the faces and the feet are the other people."

Tess nodded. "Anything else?"

"I'd say he's artistic. I can't draw like that."

"Yes, the whole thing's very intricate."

"Is that good?"

"I don't use the terms *good* or *bad*. People are what they are." Tess tapped one of the faces with a forefinger.

"Looks like the glasses and the mustache were added after the rest of the drawing was finished."

"Does that mean something?"

"Probably that our doodler craves authority and doesn't have much." She pointed to the feet beneath the line. "Look how small . . . suggests he feels insecure."

"That makes sense. Karl's twenty-four. He's probably low man on the totem pole at most meetings." Jennie was beginning to think this was too easy.

Tess smiled but didn't comment. She looked again at the drawing. "Look how angular most of his lines are. Could mean irresolution in some area of his life. And see the variety of slants? He's ambivalent about something."

Jennie wasn't sure she agreed. She said, "We aren't talking about a bunch of random lines. It's a drawing. He had to slant his lines different ways to create a picture."

Tess was staring at the picture. "I have a feeling this young man has a problem beginning a new relationship."

Jennie had to laugh at that. "If he does, he hides it well."

Tess narrowed her eyes and tilted her head. "How old did you say he is?"

"Twenty-four."

"Borderline."

"Borderline what?"

"In graphology, we set the age of maturity at about twenty-five. Before that, a person is still growing and changing, still influenced by outside events."

"Isn't everyone?"

Before Tess had a chance to answer, the door burst

open, and Leda Barrons charged in. She ignored Tess and spoke to Jennie. "I need to talk to you. Immediately."

Since it was unheard of in Riverview culture for someone to enter a resident's personal space without knocking, Jennie knew it was serious.

Chapter Twenty-one

J ennie weighed her options as she trailed along behind Leda. There was no doubt in her mind that Brooke Newton's article was behind this surprise visit. Adverse publicity for Riverview Manor was a personal affront to its Executive Director. The obvious course would be to stick to her story and ride it out—if she could, which was doubtful. It hadn't been hard to bluster her way through with Alice, but Leda was a different kind of a cat. Jennie considered telling the truth and getting it over with. That was probably the best idea, but it would mean leaving Nate hanging in the wind. *I can't do that.* She told herself it wouldn't be so bad to lose this job. At the moment she wasn't being paid anyway, and she sure couldn't afford to work for nothing. Even peanut butter and jelly cost money.

They came to the office. Leda marched in, then stopped, obviously taken aback when she saw Alice sitting at her desk. She cleared her throat. "Alice, do you mind? I need to speak with Jennifer in confidence."

Alice folded the newspaper she'd been reading and scampered for the door. She shot Jennie a pitying look on her way out.

Jennie stood with her back to the door and flinched when she heard the latch click as it swung shut. She studied Leda, prepared for the worst. Her expression was nothing like what Jennie had expected. Neither was anything else about her. She looked at least ten years older than the last time Jennie had seen her. There were dark circles under her eyes. She wore no makeup. The buttons of her pale gray silk blouse weren't in the proper holes. Jennie clasped her hands behind her back to keep from reaching out to reposition them.

"Sit down."

Jennie complied.

Leda herself did not sit but paced the area behind her desk. She stopped, looked at Jennie, opened her mouth, then closed it again and resumed pacing.

It's worse than I thought. Unwilling to wait for the ax to fall, Jennie said, "About the boat incident . . ." Midway into what had started as an explanation, Jennie felt the equivalent of an explosion in her chest. "If you're going to blame me for what happened to the reporter, don't. You put Alice in charge of a job you knew she couldn't do. So I'm stuck trying to do my job and hers, too . . . which is really yours. And, the way things stand, I'm not even getting paid." *There! I said it out loud.*

Jennie's words didn't seem to register. Leda went to the door, put her ear against it as though listening, then came back. Still, she did not sit. "Preston is going to confess."

"What?" Jennie wasn't sure she'd heard right.

Leda did not clarify.

"I don't understand. 'Confess'? You mean—"

"He's going to confess to the murder of Rob Payton."

"Preston murdered Rob?"

"Of course he didn't." A glimmer of the old Leda surfaced. She glared at Jennie. "He has some misguided idea that he has to save Web." She put her hands over her face.

Jennie noted the chipped nail polish, one nail broken and jagged. It was the first time she'd seen those hands with less than a perfect manicure. She knew Leda was crying and wondered what to do. Common decency said to comfort her. But how? She couldn't think of anything to say. A hug was out of the question. Leda Barrons was not a person Jennie could imagine hugging.

Leda removed her hands from her face and turned her back. She remained that way for what seemed an eternity. Her hands dangled at her sides, fists clenching and unclenching.

A soft knock distracted Jennie. She went to the door and spoke through it. "Can you come back later?"

Whoever it was left without comment. The only sound was the tap of retreating footsteps.

Jennie had no idea what to do, so she waited.

Finally Leda turned. She picked up a notepad and slapped the desk with it. "I don't know if I'm more frightened or angry."

Jennie tried to think of a response.

Leda apparently didn't expect one. "I'm furious with Preston because he believes our son stole that money and then committed a murder to cover it up." She turned again, a full rotation, and faced Jennie. Her face was contorted with emotion.

Jennie extended a hand. She still couldn't quite manage a hug. "Why does Preston think he did that?"

Leda moved before Jennie's hand reached hers. "I don't know. He's always been willing to believe the worst about Web."

"But he adores him."

"Yes, he does." Leda's voice cracked. When she was able to speak again, it was in reverent tones. "Preston was well into his forties when Web was born. He was thrilled to have a son." Her face became lit by an expression that hinted at a younger, softer Leda than Jennie had ever seen. The moment passed. Leda went on, "You're right. He does adore his son, so much so that he can't tolerate anything less than perfection from him. Web makes the slightest misstep, and Preston thinks the sky is falling. He's been that way since Web was a tiny child."

Jennie remembered her breakfast with Woody and his mother, Dorothea's, assessment of Preston as a father: *Expected him to be a man when he was no more than a baby.* She went to Leda, put an arm around her shoulders, and steered her to her chair. "Sit down."

Leda offered no resistance.

Still having no clear idea of what she should do, Jennie sat down herself and stared across the desk, then did the mental equivalent of jumping off a bridge into icy water. "Tell me what happened. Start at the beginning." Even as she spoke, she realized the irony of the role reversal. Another time she might have found it amusing. Today it was surreal.

Leda's eyes were fixed on a picture resting on the corner of her desk—a family portrait showing her, Preston, and Web looking like the all-American family. She didn't speak.

This could go on forever. Jennie had always laughed at her mother's dictum: "When all else fails, feed 'em." This morning it made as much sense as anything else did. She dialed the kitchen. "Please send two cups of coffee to Leda's office as soon as possible . . . and a couple pieces of toast."

Leda picked up the photograph, caressed the frame with her fingertips, and began to speak. "Preston woke me early this morning. I was surprised to see he was already dressed. He was wearing his blue suit with a striped tie." Her words came out unnaturally clear and spaced a little too far apart.

Jennie found that more upsetting than if Leda had started screaming.

Leda droned on. "I thought I'd overslept. I looked at the clock. It was six-twenty. I wondered—"

A knock startled her into silence.

Jennie went to the door, opened it enough to accept the tray, and ignored the look of the kitchen aide who delivered it. "Thanks." She closed the door and set the tray on the desk.

Leda reached for the cup nearest her and choked on her first sip.

Jennie said. "We can talk after we finish." She tasted her coffee, wondering what to do. She considered calling the staff psychologist. *It's Wednesday. He'll be in today.* She glanced at her watch. 8:55. He wouldn't arrive until after nine. *Should I get a message to him?*

Leda set her cup onto the desk with a grimace. "We have to do something about our coffee."

"Yeah, we do." Jennie almost laughed aloud with relief. If Leda could complain about the coffee, she'd survive. She set her mug beside Leda's. "Want to tell me the rest?"

Leda leaned back. "As I was saying, Preston woke me this morning, dressed as though ready to leave for the bank. He sat on the bed and asked if I'd slept well." Tears welled in her eyes. Her voice was shaky, but at least now she sounded human.

Jennie reached for a tissue from the box on the credenza and handed it to her.

Leda touched the corners of each eye. "He was very sweet, unbelievably gentle." She looked directly at Jennie for the first time. "He can be, you know. He seems stern to people who don't know him well, but Preston really is a dear man." She dabbed her eyes again and squared her shoulders. "He brought my robe and draped it around me. Then . . ." She swallowed and bit her lip. "That's when he said it."

Jennie prompted, "Said what? Exactly?"

"He said I should go away for a few days and take Web with me. I asked why. He said he was going to call that policeman."

"Lieutenant Masoski?"

"Yes. Anyway, he was going to make an appointment to see him and confess to the murder."

"Is it possible he really did it?" Jennie hated to ask but felt she had to.

Leda answered her with a withering look.

"If he said—"

"No!" Leda interrupted. "Don't you see? He *didn't* say he murdered Rob. He said he was going to confess that he had, never that he actually did. I've gone over it a thousand times, and I know what he said." She leaned closer. "Can't you see the difference?"

"Yes, but I don't understand the why of it."

"I told you. He believes Web is guilty, and he's sacrificing himself for his son. Our son." She leaned back, the old Leda restored. Two seconds later she wilted again. "And if he does confess, the police will be so pleased, they won't question it. They'll accept the confession, and Preston will spend the rest of his life in prison."

Jennie didn't believe it could be that cut-and-dry. "They'll run DNA tests, that sort of thing."

Leda bounced up from her chair. "Yes! That's why I'm so concerned. Preston's DNA is all over the murder scene. It's his office. The gun belongs to him. Even without a confession, there'd be enough evidence to convince any jury."

Leda's reasoning made sense, but Jennie wondered where she fit in. "Why are you telling me this?"

"For the same reason Preston and I came to you in the first place, when we asked you to go to the bank and look for evidence. You have a knack for what I believe is called 'thinking outside the box.' I want you to find out who killed Rob Payton and transferred the Gala funds. Use any means you have to." Having delivered her message, Leda reached for a piece of toast.

Great! Now, in addition to being an unpaid Activities Director, I'm an unpaid private detective to the richest family in Memphis.

Before Jennie had time to come up with a response,

Leda said, "If you get into trouble, I'll see to it that Hamilton gets you out of it." She nibbled the edge of the toast.

The mention of the lawyer's name prompted Jennie to ask, "Have you talked to Mr. Sunderson about this?"

Leda shook her head.

"I think you should. His advice would be better than mine." Even as she made the suggestion, Jennie understood its weakness. Hamilton Sunderson could handle the legal aspects, but Leda at this moment was driven by emotion, and Sunderson was not a man Jennie herself would go to with an emotional problem.

Leda, however, seemed to think the idea brilliant. She sat up straighter and smiled for the first time. "Of course. I'll discuss this with him." After the briefest hesitation she added, "I still want you to find the criminal." She pushed her phone across the desk toward Jennie. "Call him. Find out when he can see us."

Us?

Chapter Twenty-two

After Jennie called Sunderson, she replaced the phone and turned to Leda. "I have a couple of things to check before we go. Do you want to wait here?"

Leda, nearly restored to her usual self, fumed. "I can't believe Hamilton won't see us until one. Doesn't he know this is an emergency?"

"How could he? You wouldn't let me tell him why you wanted to see him." When Leda didn't answer, Jennie asked again, "Want to wait here?"

"I suppose I might as well. I don't want to see anyone, though."

"I'll tell Alice to make sure you're not disturbed."

"Don't tell her why. And don't breathe a word of what I've told you to anyone. Understand?"

"Yes, I understand." Jennie knew that when Leda said *understand,* she really meant *promise.* Her choice of words was just as well, because, while Jennie did understand, she wasn't prepared to promise. While she didn't really believe either Preston or Web had murdered Rob Payton, she didn't share Leda's certainty. She needed help to sort it out. Her mind was on the note Web had written to Dorothea.

She used the intercom to page Alice and arranged to meet her in the Activities Room. When Alice showed up, Jennie said, "Leda isn't feeling well. She's going to lie down on the sofa in her office. Please see that she isn't disturbed."

"Is there anything I should do? Does she need a doctor? Should I call Woody?" Concern was apparent in every flutter of Alice's hands.

"No, she just has a headache. I think she's worn out from everything that's been going on. I suggested she take a nap."

"Good idea." Alice looked relieved that nothing was expected of her.

Jennie retrieved her purse and headed for Tess's room, confident no one would disturb Leda. They wouldn't dare. No one except her knew the lioness was missing her bite today.

She passed Nate in the hall and was grateful that he was too busy regaling a young volunteer to stop her.

Tess was alone in her room, jabbing at the lock on her jewelry box with a knitting needle.

"What're you doing?" Jennie asked.

"I like to keep in practice." Tess smiled when the lid sprang open.

Jennie was too preoccupied to ask for more of an explanation. She closed the door behind her. "I need your advice."

Tess put the jewelry box and the needle aside.

Jennie removed a dog-eared paper from her purse and handed it to Tess. "This is a note written by Web a couple of years ago. What can you tell from the handwriting?"

Tess accepted the envelope from Jennie's hand but studied Jennie's face instead of the note. "Something's happened."

Jennie nodded. "I can't tell you what."

Tess cocked an eyebrow.

"Please don't ask."

The older woman turned her attention to the note. After a short perusal she said, "Very disorganized script style." She held the page out for Jennie to see. "No consistency at all, not in slant, size, or formation. That indicates instability. This person tends toward erratic behavior, is unpredictable, probably even to himself. Look at his capital letter—not much bigger than the lowercase ones. The personal pronoun is particularly telling. No follow-through in the lower loop—a sure sign of serious issues in the subject's relationship with his father."

Jennie looked. The letters were as Tess had described them. Curious, she asked, "How about the mother? Any clue to his relationship with her?"

Tess pointed to the top loop of an *I*. "Extremely sharp angle. I'd say there's stress."

"Okay," Jennie said. "Keep those things in mind. I have something else." She rummaged in her purse again. "Can you tell anything from this?" She handed Tess the map Preston had drawn for her. "I know it's not much to work with, but there's a little bit of writing." She pointed to the names Preston had written and to the corner where he had scrawled the guard's schedule.

Tess said, "You're right. It's not much, but what we have is telling." Again she focused on the personal pronoun. She traced a capital *I* with a fingertip. "Look how tall these letters are—indication of a strong ego. Notice the sharp, angular strokes. A proud person wrote this. Proud to the point of arrogance. Beginnings of letters are missing. No patience with anything that wastes time or energy." She studied the paper a little longer. "There's a nice vertical loop in the *C*. In spite of a strong ego, this person has a sense of responsibility toward others."

Jennie was impressed. "You got a lot from just those few names and numbers. I was afraid there wasn't enough to tell you anything."

Tess sat straighter. "I've had to work with less."

"Thanks for your help," Jennie said. "The things you said agree with my impression of those two people. There's something else, though."

Tess waited.

Jennie wasn't sure she should ask the next question, but it was too important not to ask. "Please don't mention this conversation to anybody," she began, then went on in a rush. "Is either of those people capable of murder?"

"In the right circumstances, anyone is capable of anything."

Jennie needed more than that. "If you had to guess, which would you say is the more likely to kill someone?"

Tess fingered her top sweater button. "I'm inclined to think the first."

"Why?"

"Because of the strong element of unpredictability."

While Tess talked, Jennie paced in the narrow space between the bed and the two chairs.

Tess reached out to her. "Sit down." When Jennie complied, she said, "I know we're dealing with something sensitive here. I suspect you've been sworn to secrecy—"

Jennie interrupted. "I didn't swear, but, yes, secrecy is important, and, since you know whose writing you've been analyzing, you can guess pretty much what's going on." She looked into Tess's eyes. "I'm in the middle of something bigger than I am, and, frankly, I don't know what to do. I'm trying to feel my way through it."

"I can see that. My advice . . ." Tess tilted her head and offered a sly smile. "This comes from many years with the Bureau. Sometimes you have to trust your instinct. Not a very modern tool, but it's the best we have." She waited for Jennie's smile, then reached out to pat her arm. "You'll do fine, dear. Your instincts are as good as any I've seen."

Jennie put her hand over Tess's and squeezed. "I hope you're right." She started to rise.

"Wait," Tess said. "Sit quietly for a few minutes. Sometimes stillness works wonders." With that, she picked up her knitting and turned away.

Jennie leaned back, closed her eyes, and tried to sort through the tangle in her head. The only sound was the click of Tess's knitting needles. She had hoped Tess would say she didn't believe either Preston or Web was capable of murder. Her answer had been that both, under the right circumstances, might be, with Web the more likely. That jibed with Margaret Payton's conviction that Web had stolen the money and then killed Rob to cover the theft. And what had Tess said about Preston's capital

C's? His vertical loops indicated a strong sense of responsibility. So he might take the blame for his son. But was Preston right that Web was guilty? As father and employer, he had opportunity to see the boy from multiple perspectives. He should know him better than anyone. Better than his mother? Better than Dorothea Samson, who had loved and cared for him since infancy? They were both convinced of his innocence. Jennie thought of the text message. *Nobody likes a busybody.* Had Preston sent it, afraid she was getting too close to his son? Somehow, she thought he'd take a more direct approach.

Then who? Jennie remembered the cell phone on Charlotte Ellio's desk, and her unwillingness to give out the number. She needed to talk to Charlotte again. She also thought of Margaret. She'd related the whole scenario as though she'd witnessed it. *Had she?* Does Margaret have a cell phone? *Doesn't everyone?* Should she talk to Margaret again, too?

A cart with a squeaky wheel passed in the hall. *Lunch already?* Jennie opened her eyes. "What time is it?"

Tess said, "Eleven-thirty."

Jennie and Leda were due in Sunderson's office at one. She had no idea how long that would take. She'd like to see both Charlotte and Margaret this afternoon. But there was something she needed to do before that.

"Tess," she said, "you know whose writing we haven't looked at? Rob's. Surely knowing more about the victim will help us find out who killed him."

Tess looked at her like a proud mother. "You'd have made a top-notch agent." Then she wagged one finger. "But you really should have checked him out first." She pulled the folder from the drawer and selected a scant batch of papers. "It was in his trash can that you found the charred paper, right?"

"Yes."

Tess didn't speak while she arranged the few papers with Rob Payton's handwriting. She held a page out for Jennie to look at. "Look how he makes his *I* when he's using it as a personal pronoun: a single stroke."

"That means?"

"He sees himself as standing alone." She peered over her glasses, which had slipped farther down on her nose, and selected another paper. "This is interesting." She held up a scrap. The amount of money raised by the Gala was written on it. "The numbers are badly formed, almost illegible. That's a common trait among convicted embezzlers."

Jennie thought back to her meeting with Rob's wife. Margaret Payton had said that Lieutenant Masoski acted as if he thought Rob had taken the money. She was convinced that someone had set her husband up. But Jennie knew Masoski was no fool. Maybe Rob did transfer the money. And somebody killed him for it. Yes, she definitely wanted to speak with Margaret again.

Tess's voice broke into her concentration. "I know that look. You have a plan."

"Maybe," Jennie said. The plan was still only half-formed. She reached for the folder and selected an assortment of papers. "There's one person left whose writing you haven't looked at. Charlotte Ellio."

"Oh, I've looked at it. I was biding my time, waiting for you to ask." She ducked her head and fluttered her lashes. "I learned a long time ago not to volunteer information."

Jennie chuckled. She should have known. The past three days had taught her there was always something going on in Tess's head. "You mean you'd already gone through those writing samples?"

"Uh-huh. The ones I had." She pointed to Web's note and Preston's map. "This is the first time I've seen those two. And they are, in many respects, the most interesting."

"Okay, so what can you tell me about Charlotte Ellio?"

Tess assumed her no-nonsense face. "Not much. She probably does whatever she has to to avoid conflict. She's not above telling lies, big ones, if they suit her purpose. No qualms at all about white lies."

Jennie thought of the glitch that had caused Charlotte's computer files to disappear. Karl insisted she was not as much of a techno-dummy as she pretended to be. If he was right, where did that deception fit into the scale of lies? White? Whopper? More important, why lie about something like that? In today's world, not being computer savvy was a handicap, especially in a financial institution. Was it connected to the crimes? What motive could Charlotte have? Money? Well, she *was* looking at investment properties and facing college costs for a daughter she adored. Jennie had a lot to think about. And no time to think. She left Tess's room and headed toward the office where Leda was waiting. She strode down the hall, staring straight ahead, preoccupied with the conflicting ideas that her conversation with Tess had spurred.

Chapter Twenty-three

When Jennie headed back to the Executive Director's office, her mind was too full of the things she and Tess had discussed to pay attention to her surroundings. *Anyone could have killed Rob.* Her foot collided with something solid. She plunged forward and threw out her hands to break her fall. Most of her weight landed on her left hand, which splayed at a painful angle across the top of a large square object. Warning labels shouted danger from every visible surface. FRAGILE. EXPLOSIVES. HANDLE WITH CARE. She'd stumbled over a box. And beyond that box were at least half a dozen more. They stood in a neat row, lined up like soldiers in a firing squad, all marked with the same dire warnings.

What the—oh, the fireworks. Lucky I didn't break my neck. What idiot left them here?

She detoured and went looking for Alice and found her in the Activities Room, playing Scrabble with Doreen.

The peaceful tableau only served to stoke Jennie's anger. She told herself to cool it. Alice's hold on the temporary authority she'd had to shoulder was precarious enough. Jennie forced the corners of her mouth upward. "Alice, can we talk?"

She directed a more genuine smile toward Doreen. "This won't take long."

Doreen said, "Don't worry about it." She looked closely at Jennie, who was clutching her wrist, holding it straight. "What's wrong?"

"I fell. Messed up my wrist."

"You should have one of the nurses look at it."

Alice, who didn't seem to hear Doreen's comments, followed Jennie into the hall. Her mouth was twitching like an anxious squirrel. "Is Leda feeling worse?"

"No, this has nothing to do with Leda. Some idiot left boxes filled with fireworks out in the hall." She threw out her hands to demonstrate—a big mistake. A shaft of pain shot up to her elbow.

"Is that what's got you so worked up? I told the deliverymen to leave them there."

"You're kidding!" The throbbing in her wrist didn't improve Jennie's disposition.

"Do you have a better idea?"

Jennie flexed her wrist and winced. "They're supposed to take them out to the shed on the island."

"I know, but they were shorthanded today, so they left them up here. I said it would be okay."

It didn't sound okay to Jennie. "What if a resident stumbles over a box? I just did."

Alice finally seemed to notice Jennie holding her wrist. "It's really bothering you, isn't it?"

"Not half as much as the thought of one of the residents falling over a box."

Alice gave Jennie a kind but beleaguered look. "They don't go racing through the halls like you do."

Jennie moved on to a more pressing concern. "What if there's an accident, and the fireworks are ignited?"

"What are the chances of that? Are they really that sensitive?"

"Probably not. Still, it's dangerous to have those big boxes in the hall."

"It's only until tomorrow."

Jennie told herself to go slowly. Alice's feelings were already hurt. She changed tack. "It's your call. When I stumbled into that box and saw warnings plastered all over it . . ."

Alice stood there nodding, her expression one of patience and understanding.

A kick in the shins would have been less infuriating. Jennie gulped down her first choice of words and said, "Something to think about—what if a safety inspector or someone from the Board of Health stops by unannounced?" Jennie could see that she had Alice's attention now, so she pressed forward, but in a gentler tone. "You might want to get someone to at least move the boxes out of the hall." She tried to disarm Alice with a smile. "I don't envy you this job. It's overwhelming to step in on such short notice. You must feel like the proverbial one-armed paperhanger."

Alice seemed mollified. "I'll take care of the boxes. By the way, how's Leda?"

"I was on my way to check on her when I saw the fireworks. I wouldn't be surprised if the nap revived her and she'll be heading home soon." She gave Alice another smile. "You'll probably be back in that office before lunch is over." She turned to go and remembered that Alice was now—technically, at least—her boss. "Leda asked me to run an errand with her, so I'll be out of the building for a while, maybe the rest of the day. You okay with that?"

Alice seemed pleased to be asked. "We'll be fine here. You just take care of little Leda." That was the closest Alice had ever come to criticizing Leda, though Leda browbeat Alice in subtle ways all the time.

Jennie didn't comment. She merely smiled and said, "Thanks."

Alice waved her off. "You should take time to let someone look at your wrist."

"I will." Jennie left the problem of the fireworks to Alice and went to see what Leda was up to. When she reached the door marked EXECUTIVE DIRECTOR, she tapped lightly.

There was no response.

"Leda? It's me, Jennie."

"Come in." Leda was seated with her back to the door, looking out into the courtyard. She turned as Jennie entered the room and looked meaningfully at her watch. "Where have you been?"

"A resident was feeling a little neglected. I stopped by her room for a chat." Not a lie, Jennie told herself.

"I should think you'd have more immediate concerns right now."

"The residents are my job."

"I asked you to find out who committed these terrible crimes. That should be your highest priority."

Jennie marveled at the change in Leda's demeanor.

Maybe she really had taken a nap. Maybe the prospect of transferring the burden to her lawyer's shoulders had revived her. Whatever the reason, she was her old, domineering self. "You might want to have lunch pretty soon," Jennie said. "It's almost twelve now, and we're supposed to meet Mr. Sunderson at one." She held up her arm. "I did something to my wrist. You can grab something from the dining room while I have a nurse look at it."

Leda looked annoyed. "Can it wait 'til later?" Without waiting for an answer, she grabbed her purse. "If you're hungry, we can stop somewhere. I don't want to eat here."

Jennie told herself the wrist would be fine. It didn't seem worth an argument. Not now. Leda was keyed up enough already. They walked together to the back parking lot. When Jennie headed for her car, Leda stopped her and asked, "Think you can drive?"

"Sure," Jennie said.

"Fine. We'll go in my car."

"But then I'll be stranded downtown."

Leda waved that off. "I'll see that you get back." She handed her keys to Jennie and looked from the gleaming Mercedes to Jennie's dented VW. "It'll be easier for you to drive with that wrist than your car. I think you'll find it a nice change."

It was a change, all right. The car was a pleasure to drive, but when they hit downtown traffic, Jennie missed the Beetle's maneuverability. Hamilton Sunderson's office was in a high-rise a block from Barrons Bank and Trust. Jennie slowed down at the entrance to a parking garage around the corner from the building.

"Oh, for heaven's sake," Leda said. "Just drive to the front door. I'll have Hamilton send someone to park the car." She took her cell phone from her purse, punched in a number, spoke half a dozen words, and the matter was settled.

Jennie reflected, not for the first time, that the pleasures of money went beyond paying bills without performing a juggling routine. A little intimidated, she followed Leda up to the lawyer's office.

She'd been at Riverview meetings when Hamilton Sunderson was present, but she'd never been in his private digs before. Very imposing. Lots of mahogany, a desk that could serve as a banquet table, and miles of bookshelves. One wall was devoted to an impressive array of diplomas and awards. A sheathed sword occupied a place of honor among the framed certificates. Elaborate etching on the hilt and scabbard suggested the weapon had belonged to an officer, no doubt a leader of the once-proud Confederacy.

Sunderson rose to meet them. He held out a chair for Leda and, with a wave of his hand, invited Jennie to sit in another.

"Well," he said when he was settled behind his desk. "What's the important matter we need to discuss?"

Leda couldn't seem to find the words she needed. Finally she turned to Jennie. "You explain."

Sunderson swiveled his chair a quarter turn to face Jennie.

She plunged right in. "Preston plans to confess to transferring the Gala funds and murdering Rob Payton." *There! No use gilding the lily.*

Sunderson's expression was inscrutable. He turned to Leda and raised his eyebrows.

She nodded.

Neither of them spoke, so Jennie went on. "Leda thinks Preston believes Web did it, and he's trying to protect him."

Leda came alive. "Have you ever heard anything so ridiculous?"

Sunderson whistled through his teeth and leaned back. "Did he say when he plans to do this?"

Jennie looked toward Leda.

Leda said, "I wouldn't be surprised if he's at the station right now. This morning he seemed determined. And you know Preston—once he makes up his mind about something, he takes action." Halfway through the outburst, tears began to flow. At its end, Leda covered her face with her hands, and her shoulders began to shake.

Sunderson removed a handkerchief from his pocket and handed it across the desk to Jennie. Then he swiveled so he was facing out the window.

Jennie gave Leda the handkerchief and patted her shoulder. Rarely had she felt so inadequate.

Finally Sunderson turned back to them. He looked sternly at Leda. "We have a problem, I agree. But I'm sure your fears are exaggerated. Preston would call me before he did anything like that. At the very least, he'd ask me to accompany him to the police station."

Jennie asked, "Have you heard from him today?"

"No." He drummed his fingers on the desk. He looked as much at a loss as Leda.

After several minutes of waiting for a decision from these two high-powered individuals, Jennie said, "We could call the bank and see if he's there."

"Excellent suggestion." Sunderson pressed a button

and said, "Miss Jones, please place a call to Preston Barrons at the bank."

A clipped voice replied, "Yes, Mr. Sunderson."

The wait seemed endless. Leda unleashed a gentle hiccup that sounded like thunder in the silent office and didn't bother to excuse herself. Finally the voice came back. "Mr. Sunderson?"

"Yes?"

"Mr. Barrons isn't in, but Ms. Ellio would like to speak to you."

Sunderson and Leda exchanged looks.

Sunderson said, "Put her through." He looked toward Leda, then Jennie. "I'll use the speakerphone so you can hear. I suggest you remain quiet unless I ask you to speak."

Both nodded.

Charlotte Ellio's voice, obviously stressed, said, "Mr. Sunderson, I was about to call you to ask if you've seen Preston. He has a meeting at two o'clock, and I have questions about a report I'm preparing. He didn't come in this morning. I tried his home. Leda isn't there either, and the household staff doesn't know where either of them is."

Despite the lawyer's admonition, Leda spoke up. "Charlotte, I'm here, in Hamilton's office. Has Preston called?"

"No. I haven't heard from him all day. Neither has anyone else."

"Is our son there?"

"No, Web didn't come in this morning."

There was another exchange of looks between Leda and Sunderson. Sunderson said, "Have you tried Preston's cell phone?"

Leda looked offended and snapped, "Well, of course I have."

Charlotte's voice came over the speaker. "I've tried it several times."

Sunderson said, "Call me immediately if Preston comes in. Or if he calls you."

Leda added, "Or Web. Call if you hear from him." She took her phone from her purse and punched in a number.

Charlotte Ellio could be heard clearing her throat. "About the meeting . . . it's with some investors."

Sunderson glanced at his watch. "I suggest you cancel it."

"What if I can't reach them? They're driving over from Jackson. I'm sure they're on their way by now." She paused. "I could call their office and get their cell numbers, but, this late, they won't be happy. Usually, if Preston can't make a meeting for some reason, Rob Payton would go in his place, but . . ."

"I see your problem," Sunderson said. He thought for a few seconds. "I'll attend the meeting. Assemble any data you have, and be prepared to fill me in." As soon as that call ended, Sunderson pushed another button. "Miss Jones, clear my schedule this afternoon." He looked toward Jennie and Leda.

Leda said, "I just tried to reach Preston's cell again. There's no answer. None on Web's either."

Sunderson said, "Let's take one thing at a time. I'm going to that meeting, and, when it's over, I'll make a few phone calls and see if I can find out anything."

Jennie marveled at his changed demeanor when he rose from his chair. He looked like a young athlete, eager for the game to begin.

He opened the office door and stood beside it, a clear signal for Jennie and Leda to leave. As Leda passed him, he patted her arm. "Try not to worry. I'm sure Preston has thought better of this idea. Call me if you hear from him."

Chapter Twenty-four

Leda headed for the driver's side when the young associate from Sunderson's law firm brought the Mercedes around.

Since Jennie wasn't sure of Leda's intentions, she asked, "You want to drive me back to Riverview so I can pick up my car? Or should I take a cab?" *If so, who's going to pay for it?* Long cab rides were not in Jennie's budget, especially since she didn't know when she'd see her next paycheck.

Leda ran her thumb over the car key's ragged edge.

Jennie thought she looked embarrassed. A horn blasted. A driver shook his fist at the double-parked Mercedes and yelled something Jennie was glad she couldn't understand.

"I'd rather not go home," Leda finally said. "I don't want to be there if the police come by."

"So . . . back to Riverview?"

"No." She drew the word out. "Until I know what Preston's up to, I'd like to keep a low profile. That's not possible for me at Riverview."

Jennie hesitated, then asked, "Would you like to come to my house?"

"That would be lovely. Thank you." She handed the keys to Jennie and walked to the passenger side.

Darn! Jennie hadn't dreamed Leda would accept. It was fine, of course. Leda and Preston had been at Jennie's for dinner on several occasions. But, today, well, after a sleepless night . . . *I didn't even make the bed this morning.* She thought of the nooks and crannies where cobwebs loved to hide. As for dinner . . . *No idea what's in the fridge.* She remembered they hadn't had lunch yet and was suddenly ravenous. She looked over at Leda. "You hungry? Let's stop for a barbecue sandwich."

"I don't want to run into anyone."

"I'll get takeout from Corky's. You can wait in the car."

Leda chewed on her lower lip.

Jennie was running out of patience. She sympathized with Leda's plight, but enough was enough. "Look, I don't know what I've got at the house. It's been a rough week, and I haven't had time to hit the supermarket." She hoped Leda detected the unspoken *thanks to you and your husband* underlying her words.

If Leda did, she didn't show it. She said, "Not Corky's. Find some out-of-the-way place."

"Sure." Jennie drove another block, keeping an eye out for something, anything, and spotted a mom-and-pop barbecue stand in a strip mall. "That look okay?" She pulled in without waiting for an answer. "Coming in? Or shall I get take out?"

"Takeout's fine." Leda fished in her purse and handed

Jennie a twenty. When Jennie hesitated, she said, "For heaven's sake, don't be silly. I'm not a complete fool. I know when I'm imposing."

Jennie opened her mouth.

Leda waved her into silence. "Just go. I'm hungry, too."

The sandwiches lived up to the reputation enjoyed by Memphis barbecue, and the coleslaw had just enough vinegar to balance the smoky flavor of the sauce. After they ate, Jennie tidied up the kitchen. They spent the rest of the afternoon rehashing the events of the past few days.

Jennie brought up the matter of the two-hour time difference on Sunday night. "I still don't understand why Margaret Payton said the meeting was for midnight, and you and Preston sent me to the bank at two A.M."

"Maybe Margaret got it wrong."

Jennie watched Leda's face and body language. Both told her Leda was telling the truth. At least as she knew it. Had Margaret been wrong about the time? Or lied to Jennie about it? Or, just as possible, had Preston lied to his wife? Jennie didn't voice this doubt to Leda. She didn't see how doing so would help the situation, and it might send Leda into a frenzy Jennie wasn't prepared to deal with. Besides, there was something else she wanted to bring up.

Jennie found the notepad in her purse and showed Leda the page on which she'd written the phone number. "Do you recognize this number?" She watched Leda's face, knowing the chances were pretty good she would. Jennie had already decided the text message must have come from someone connected to the bank, and Leda had a phenomenal memory for numbers of any kind.

Leda squinted at the paper, then said, "I think it's Charlotte Ellio's cell. I usually call on the bank phone when I need to talk to her, so I'm not a hundred percent sure, but I know I've called that number. Why?"

Jennie told her about the text message.

Leda asked, "Did you tell the police about this?"

"No," Jennie said. "It's not really threatening. I'd feel kind of silly. It might not have anything to do with the murder."

"I hope you're at least being careful."

"I am," Jennie said, at the same time remembering that Leda had told her to use any means necessary to find the murderer. How careful could she be and still do that?

Leda didn't press the matter, and they spent the rest of the afternoon trying to pass the time. Jennie taught her to play Australian Rummy, and, after the first game, Leda beat her every time.

When it was time for the news, Jennie turned on the TV. There was no mention of Rob Payton's murder.

Leda said, "At least I know Preston hasn't done anything foolish yet."

"The old 'no news is good news,'" Jennie said.

The evening yawned before them. They took turns clicking the remote, but TV offered only its usual summer fare. Leda alternately dialed Preston's, then Web's, cell phone every half hour. Every time she failed to reach them, she left the same message: "Call me. Now." When her phone rang, she snatched it. "Preston?"

Jennie could tell from Leda's face, it wasn't Preston. Within seconds it was apparent she was speaking to Hamilton Sunderson, and he hadn't heard from Preston either.

When Leda hung up, Jennie asked, "How'd the meeting go?"

"Okay, I guess. He didn't have much to say. No one's heard from either Preston or Web." She stared at the blank TV screen and finally said, "I think I know what he's doing. He's just driving around, thinking, trying to come up with a plan. Probably on some country road."

"Do you think Web's with him?"

"There's a good chance he is. When Web was small, if Preston wanted to have a serious talk with him, he'd do that. Take him for a long car ride . . . said that way he had a captive audience." Leda looked more hopeful than she had all day.

"So, it might be a good sign we haven't heard from them?"

"Maybe." Leda picked up the remote again, tossed it aside, got up, and paced the room until Jennie was ready to scream.

Jennie finally suggested, "Let's go to a movie."

"I can't possibly do that. What if Preston calls? Or Web?"

"They'll use the cell. You can set it on vibrate in the theater."

Leda looked doubtful.

Jennie nudged a little. "We can't keep this up. It's like waiting for eggs to boil." She found the newspaper and flipped through it. "That new vampire movie is supposed to be good."

"Never heard of it."

"It's billed as a dark comedy."

"Sounds appropriate."

* * *

The movie took Jennie's mind off the missing bankers for sometimes as long as five minutes at a time—a big improvement over sitting at home with Leda. She looked sideways and noticed that Leda's hand was in her pocket, presumably cradling her cell phone.

Later, in the car, Jennie said, "Want to be decadent and stop for ice cream?"

"Why not?"

They stopped at a Dairy Queen, and both had Blizzards. The setting reminded Jennie of the kids and made her a little melancholy, but at least it took her mind off larger problems.

When she turned into her drive, the headlights hit a row of tools hung on the back wall of the garage. *Guess I forgot to close the door. Strange. Oh, well, no big deal.* She glanced at the car clock and was thankful it was after eleven. She and Leda could stop trying to be sociable and go to bed.

"I'll see what I can find for you to sleep in." Jennie spoke over her shoulder as she switched on the light. The garage door opened into a laundry area. Next was the kitchen, separated from the family room by a half wall. When light flooded the space, Jennie stopped, unable to breathe. She might have left the garage door open, but this—

The wing chair was overturned, its legs thrust into the air as if in protest. Sofa pillows lay in a heap by the fireplace. Desk drawers gaped open; one lay upside down in a corner. Paper littered the floor. A lamp had been knocked off an end table. Its broken bulb lay in slivers on the floor.

Jennie stared, trying to take it in. White-hot anger came

first, then cold, numbing fear. Her hands began to shake. She curled them into fists. *Thank God the kids aren't here.*

Leda spoke first. "Somebody broke in."

Obviously. Jennie pivoted to survey the rest of the room. One wall had bookshelves with baskets lining the bottom row. The baskets had been emptied of their contents and tossed about. One looked as if someone had stomped on it. Jennie bent to pick it up. Her fingers refused to grip. She sat down on the floor and put her hands between her knees in an effort to steady them. Her left wrist throbbed in protest. She looked across the room at Leda, then down the dark hallway that led to the bedrooms. *We have to get out of here.*

She got up and signaled to Leda to follow.

When they were in the car, she said, "Lock your door. Call 911." When Leda didn't respond immediately, she said, "Someone might still be in there."

Leda punched in 911 and handed the phone to Jennie.

Jennie gave her name and address and said, "There's been a break-in at my home." When the details had been exchanged, she said to Leda, "We'll stay in the car until the police come."

They waited, each lost in private thoughts. Both jumped when the interior light of the car timed out. In the dark, the previously quiet night seemed to throb with sound.

Leda pointed to the house. "Do you really think they're still in there?"

"It's not worth taking a chance." Jennie tried to gather her thoughts. She had to get this right. Finally, she turned to Leda. "I know you don't want to talk to the police. With Preston and Web missing . . ." She paused, unsure how to phrase the next bit. "If that comes up—"

"I know," Leda interrupted, "but we won't mention it unless we have to."

Jennie nodded and said, "We had to call them. There's just so much we can do by ourselves. I'm betting that whoever killed Rob Payton did this. Everyone at the bank knows I found his body while looking for something for Preston. They're worried that I found something, and they want it back, whatever it is."

"You think it was someone from the bank?"

"Face it, Leda, it has to be. Who else could transfer funds in the exact amount raised by the Gala and get into the bank in the middle of the night? It had to be someone who had a key and knew the guard's schedule. They had to know Web's computer, his password. And all about the bank's systems." What Jennie did not say was that Preston fit the profile better than anyone, with Web a close second.

In the dark car, Leda's face was a ghostly white.

Jennie looked toward the house. "It has to be the same person. And that person is a murderer." She remembered Tess's statement that the first time is the hardest and added, "They're desperate."

Chapter Twenty-five

The police car arrived with a swirl of colored light.

Jennie opened her window when a tall man with rounded shoulders got out and approached.

He tilted his head toward the house. "This where the break-in occurred?"

"Yes."

He gazed at her, as though waiting for more.

She said, "We went inside and saw what had happened, and we came right back out. I don't know if they're still in there. I didn't seen anyone, but—"

"That was smart." The cop had a fringe of graying hair sticking out from beneath his cap, and he looked about fifty. He nodded toward his partner, a much younger man, whose cheeks worked in rhythmic movement.

Jennie thought him a little strange until she realized he was sucking a lemon drop. She could smell it. It seemed odd, out of sync with the situation. Then it occurred to her how odd it was that she noticed.

The older man put a hand on Jennie's shoulder and said, "Wait in the car until we come for you."

Jennie did as she was told. It felt odd, inhospitable, sending two strangers into her house while she waited outside. She imagined them walking through, entering each room. They were still inside when the lights of another car hit the rearview mirror, momentarily blinding her. She watched a short, stockily built man exit the newly arrived vehicle and walk toward them.

He shone a flashlight into her face. "You okay?"

She knew that voice. Lieutenant Masoski was here. For once, she was glad to see him. "I had a break-in."

"So I heard." He directed the beam to Leda and grunted when he saw who it was. "You two hang out a lot?"

Leda said, "We went to a movie."

He shone his light around the garage, then back to Jennie's face. "Where's your car? Burglars steal it?"

She shielded her eyes with one hand and, with the other, pointed toward the door. "The light switch is over there."

He turned on the overhead light. "Your car?"

"I left it at Riverview Manor."

"Any reason?" His tone was conversational, as though he were just passing the time.

Jennie knew better. "We didn't need both cars." She imitated his casual manner.

He chewed on his lower lip. "You two go to a movie together. Your house is broken into. A few nights ago, you were in a bank owned by this lady's family. A body was discovered. Looks like a pattern."

Every response that sprang to Jennie's mind seemed likely to get her into trouble, so she remained silent.

Masoski turned his attention to Leda. "Mr. Barrons on his way?"

"I haven't called him." Leda smiled. "I'm sure you and your men can handle everything."

He smiled back. "If it were my wife, I'd want to know."

The words Leda and Masoski exchanged were innocent enough, but it was clear to Jennie that they were sparring. The homicide cop obviously felt there was something off about Leda's presence and was taking tentative jabs to find out what. Leda held her own, showing enough toughness to hold him off, not so much that she antagonized him. Jennie marveled at her presence of mind, especially considering the strain she was under.

The young cop appeared at the back door. "Hey, Stan, you coming in?"

"In a minute." He didn't take his eyes off Leda. "Your husband called, made an appointment to see me tomorrow. Any idea what that's about?"

"No." Leda's voice was flat, impervious.

Masoski didn't pursue it. "Wait here." He left them alone and went into the house. After about ten minutes he came to the door and waved them in.

Jennie, Leda, and Masoski joined the two other policemen in the trashed family room.

Masoski asked, "Anything missing?"

"I don't know," Jennie said. "When we came in and saw this, we went right back out and called 911."

Masoski studied Jennie. "Somebody was looking for something. Any idea what?"

Jennie repeated what she'd told Leda earlier. "My guess is the killer wonders if I found anything at the bank that would implicate them."

"Did you?"

"Not that I know of. I didn't take time to examine the stuff. I just took it with me." She met his gaze. "You have it now."

"All of it?"

"Yes."

"You didn't withhold anything?"

She threw up her hands and rolled her eyes. "Not a thing."

Masoski spread his arms toward the mess on the floor. "Can you tell if anything's missing?"

Jennie nudged a fan of bank statements with her toe. "Chances are, I won't know what's missing until I need it."

"Do a quick look-through without touching anything."

She knelt at the edge of the sea of paper and listed items as they caught her eye: "Checkbook, bank statements, bills, address book, stamps, postcards from the kids, coupons . . . oh!"

"What?" Masoski moved closer and peered over her shoulder.

"There's an earring." She pointed to the leaf-shaped clip-on. "It's not mine," Jennie looked at Leda to see if she was missing an earring. No, both of Leda's ears sported diamond studs.

Masoski followed Jennie's gaze. He picked the earring up and held it out toward Leda. "Recognize this?"

Leda examined it. "No."

Masoski turned to the other two cops. "Either of you seen this before?"

"No."

"Not mine." The older cop sounded amused.

"Okay." Masoski smiled as he pocketed the earring. He asked Jennie, "Who at the bank knows where you live?"

"I'm listed in the phone book. And I imagine after last weekend, everyone knows my name."

"Any strange phone calls lately? Other suspicious activity?"

She hesitated. "One thing. I don't know if it's suspicious. Someone left me a text message saying 'Nobody likes a busybody.' "

"Did you recognize the number?"

Jennie looked at Leda. "No. I wrote it down. Leda thinks it belongs to Charlotte Ellio."

"You still have the paper you wrote it on?"

Jennie nodded, found the scrap of paper, and handed it to Masoski.

He stuffed it into his pocket. "When was this?"

So much had happened over the past few days, Jennie's perception of time was distorted. It took her a moment to place the message in the right time frame. "Yesterday."

"Why didn't you tell me this before?"

"I didn't know if it was important—"

"Next time, call. I'll decide what's important." He crossed his arms and asked, "Anything else?"

"The other night—last night, actually—I came home from Riverview late, and I thought someone might be following me."

"How late?"

"A little after ten."

"You didn't report this either?"

"I wasn't sure. It was just . . . there was a car behind me most of the way, and there's usually not much traffic."

Masoski's eyes were directed at Jennie but seemed to be looking through her. After a long couple of minutes he looked down at the floor. "We'll go through this together. But not tonight. I want someone from the department to examine the place first." He turned a grim face to Jennie and Leda. "You're sure you haven't disturbed anything? Except for this?" He held out his hand with the earring in its palm.

"No. Like I told you, when I saw what had happened, I got out of here."

Leda shook her head.

Masoski said, "Okay. I'll have someone out first thing tomorrow." He paced the perimeter of the room, his hands in his pockets. "We'll look for fingerprints and anything your intruder may have left behind. Then I need you to go over some things with me. Meet me here around one." He stopped pacing to look at her. "You shouldn't stay here tonight."

"I know."

"You have some place to go?"

Leda said, "She's staying with me. I wouldn't think of leaving her alone after this." She looked at the paper-strewn floor, the tipped-over chair.

Masoski nodded. He turned to the older cop. "Secure the premises. One of you stay here tonight. Call me if you see or hear anything funny." He looked at Jennie and Leda. "You two can go." Then, to Jennie, he added, "One o'clock tomorrow." He handed her a card. "Call me if anything comes up." He brought the earring out of his pocket and held it up. "No need to mention this to anyone. Understand?"

Jennie and Leda both nodded.

Masoski turned away. The dismissal was obvious.

Back in the car, Jennie said, "There's probably a couple of empty beds at Riverview. We can crash there."

"Not an option." Leda was adamant.

"Your house?"

"No. I'll get us hotel rooms."

Jennie still had the keys to the Mercedes. She started the car and asked, "Where to?"

"The Peabody. We'll be safe there."

It was a quiet ride. Both women were lost in their own thoughts. Jennie couldn't help wondering why Preston still hadn't called. And how had the burglar known the house would be empty tonight? That led to still other thoughts, best left unexplored.

Chapter Twenty-six

Jennie tried to punch her pillow into shape. It didn't work; something wasn't right. Conscious she was in a strange place, she opened her eyes. The room was semi-dark. The sheets were smooth, but the smell was wrong—pleasant but not the lavender potpourri of home. Then it came to her; she was at the Peabody. Her house had been broken into. Violated. The memory brought full wakefulness.

She looked at the wall separating her room from the one next door and wondered if Leda was awake. She scanned the area until she saw a clock. Almost 7:30. She started to sit up. Pain shot up her arm from her left wrist, reminding her of the boxes in Riverview's hallway. Since tonight was the big celebration, surely the fireworks had been moved out to the island by now. Jennie's head reeled at the thought of all she had to do. She had to go through the house with Lieutenant Masoski, but not until one. In the meantime, she'd go to work and try to act normal. See what happened next. *And watch my back.*

Shadows of a dream that had recurred off and on all night came back to her: a tree—no, not a tree, a single leaf, an elongated oval, like a birch leaf, something like that. Not a bad image. Why was it threatening? Ah—the earring she'd found on her floor last night, the one foreign object in a familiar place. Everything else, scattered though it had been, at least belonged in her home. The earring was a link to the invader. There was something elusive, just out of her mind's reach about its size and shape. It hadn't been in her hand long before she turned it over to Masoski, but the look and feel of it were imprinted on her brain.

She picked up a notepad from the bedside table and scrounged in the drawer until she found a stubby pencil. She started to sketch, allowing her mind and hand free rein, and was able to recreate the earring, full-size, on the small paper.

She leaned back in the pillows to study the drawing. Had she ever seen Leda with an earring like that? No. Leda always wore diamond studs. Someone at the bank? Probably. Okay, who? Charlotte? Or what about Margaret Payton?

She forced herself to recall details of Charlotte's person yesterday, when they'd had their harried lunch date. She'd been disheveled, her clothing in disarray. Jewelry? Jennie recalled the earring found on the floor next to Charlotte's desk. This earring? Jennie stared at the drawing. She closed her eyes, willing the image into sharper focus. Charlotte had been wearing blue, and the earring was a blue enamel shape. So that wasn't where Jennie had seen this particular earring—if she had, indeed, seen it. Margaret? *Hmm, could be.* A ringing telephone shattered her concentration.

"Hello."

Leda's voice: "Did you sleep at all?"

"Yes. Did you?"

Leda's answer was a vague single syllable, which Jennie took to mean "no."

Jennie asked, "Have you heard anything from Preston? Or Web?"

"No." Nothing vague about that response. This morning Leda sounded more angry than worried about her husband and son. "We're going to find them," Leda said. "I have a plan. We'll talk about it over breakfast. Here in my room. I'll call room service. What would you like?"

Jennie didn't ask about Leda's plan. She knew it wouldn't mesh with her own. "Sorry. Can't do it. I have to leave for Riverview in fifteen minutes at the most."

Leda's reaction was quick and unequivocal. "Nonsense. After last night, no one will expect—"

"No one but us, and the burglar knows about that. If we keep it that way, maybe he—"

"Or she," Leda interrupted. "Remember the earring."

"Right," Jennie said. "We need to keep the appearance of normality. Besides, remember what today is?" When there was no answer, Jennie prompted, "Fourth of July. I have to be there."

Leda didn't argue. She did suggest, "At least have breakfast. Make an excuse about oversleeping."

"No. I'll grab a quick shower, then take off. I'll call you if I learn anything. And you call me if you hear from Preston."

Again, there was no argument. Leda said, "All right. Good luck,"—just a tic of hesitation, then—"I appreciate all you've done."

Jennie savored Leda's contrite tone but refrained from rubbing it in. "We both want things back to normal as soon as possible. I have to get going." She paused, hoping Leda would remember that she didn't have a car. When she didn't, Jennie reminded her. "My car's still at Riverview. Okay if I take yours?"

Leda said, "I can't be without a car. Preston might call and ask me to meet him. Have the doorman get a cab for you."

"I don't have money to pay for a cab ride all the way out there."

"Stop by my room. I have enough cash. It's the least I can do."

Jennie agreed but thought it would be ungracious to say so. "Thanks."

Jennie noted that the boxes were gone from the hallway and wondered whom Alice had shanghaied into moving them.

In the dining hall, she looked toward the corner table where the tea ladies usually held court. There they were, all six of them. Georgie was waving her arms, obviously telling a story—a juicy one, judging from the expressions of the other ladies.

Jennie exchanged hasty greetings with residents and staff as she made her way to them. "Mind if I join you?"

Georgie paused long enough to say, "The more the merrier."

Jennie pulled over a chair from another table, and

Doreen moved her wheelchair to make space. When Jennie sat down, Georgie resumed her story, something scandalous about a well-known Memphis politician. Jennie heard the words without listening. She tried to signal Tess, who was seated across the table, that she wanted to talk to her. Alone.

Doreen said, "You look tired. I'm afraid with everything going on, you're not getting enough sleep."

Jennie said, "I'm supposed to look after you, not vice versa."

With Doreen's comment, the other ladies turned to study Jennie.

"You do look tired, dear." Their voices, as so often happened, overlapped and braided into a common concern.

Tess came up with a practical suggestion. "How about breakfast?"

"I'm not hungry." A small pitcher of maple syrup in the center of the table sent an aromatic message. On second thought, breakfast did sound appealing. Jennie looked toward the kitchen, then back at the ladies. "French toast?"

"Yes," in chorus.

"I'll see if I can scrounge some leftovers." On her way to the kitchen, she saw Alice in the hall talking to a tall, broad-shouldered man. *Nice.* Jennie looked closer. From the back he was a dead ringer for Karl Erickson.

Alice noticed her and waved.

The man turned around. Sure enough, it was Karl. When he saw Jennie, he started toward her. Alice came with him. When they reached Jennie, Alice gushed, "This young man is a lifesaver."

Karl rolled his eyes and tried to look modest.

Jennie asked, "What'd he do?"

"You know those boxes you were so upset about yesterday? Well, he moved them for us. Did it all by himself."

"Good. I'm glad they're out of the hall." Jennie looked at Karl. "I almost broke my neck." She flexed the bad wrist and winced.

"What's wrong?" Karl asked.

Alice answered for her. "She fell over the boxes."

"My turn for a question," Jennie said. She looked at Karl. "What're you doing here? Don't you have plans for the holiday?"

"I was kind of hoping somebody here would invite me to see the fireworks."

Alice said, "You've earned at least that."

Karl smiled his thanks at Alice but focused on Jennie. "What time?"

"Dusk, but the party starts around five. Right after supper, there's a band concert."

When Jennie and Karl continued to talk without including her, Alice drifted away.

Karl said, "Have time for coffee?"

"Actually, I was on my way to the kitchen to see if I could cadge some leftover French toast when I saw you."

"Mind if I join you? Maybe you can talk somebody out of a cup of coffee for me."

They settled at a table near the patio doors. The tea ladies were leaving. When Tess passed, Jennie said, "Okay if I stop by in a little bit?"

"That'll be fine. We can work on our project."

"What's the project?" Karl asked.

"Nothing special," Jennie said. She was having trouble cutting the toast into bites because of her wrist.

"Let me help." Karl reached for the plate and knocked

Jennie's purse off the table. He flashed that heart-stopping lopsided grin and leaned over to pick up the purse and its contents. He laid everything on the table. "I'll let you put it all back."

"Good idea." She watched him cut her breakfast into bite-size pieces and dug in when he finished. Between bites she asked, "How're things at the bank?" She hoped she sounded casual.

He deadpanned, "Well, there's been a murder."

"I know that. Anything else?"

"Now it seems our fearless leader has disappeared."

"No kidding. Anybody have any idea where he is?"

"That's partly why I'm here. No one's been able to reach Preston. Or any of the family. We hoped, since Leda works here, you folks might know where they are. I volunteered to come check it out."

"Leda's missing, too?"

"Well, she's not taking phone calls. Nobody can get past Dorothea. You know where they are?"

"No." Jennie said it without hesitation, telling herself it was only a third of a lie and maybe not even that. Who knew if Leda was still at the Peabody?

Karl sat quietly, looking bored, alternately watching Jennie eat and gazing around the room. He reached toward the pile of things that had fallen out of her purse. "You picky about how these go in, or can I scoop them in for you?"

"I wouldn't say I'm picky, but I don't want everything just scooped in either."

"Okay." He started to pull his hand back, stopped midway, and reached for the notepad with the drawing of the earring. "You do this?"

"Yes."

"Nice."

"Just a doodle."

"I'm a doodler, too. This is good. Great detail." He leaned forward and examined the side of Jennie's face. "Can't be one of yours. You have pierced ears."

Jennie forgot about food. That's what had bothered her about the earring. It was a clip-on. Almost everyone she knew had pierced ears. She remembered she'd promised Masoski she wouldn't tell anyone about the earring found amid the wreckage of her house and changed the subject. "Did Roger find the backup for Charlotte's computer files?"

"Don't think so. Of course, she doesn't confide in me." He looked as if he was uncertain if he should go on. "What have you learned about Charlotte?" When Jennie didn't answer, he added, "Come on, you're not going to pretend you haven't been investigating all of us who were connected to Rob?"

"Is Charlotte connected to Rob? I mean, other than the fact that they both worked for Preston?"

"You really don't know, do you?"

"Please, no cat and mouse. What don't I know?"

"Have dinner with me, and I'll tell you."

Jennie didn't respond.

"Sorry, that was out of line. I take it back. Rob and Charlotte had a little fling about a year ago."

Jennie sputtered her coffee. "You're kidding!"

He shook his head.

"She's—what—how many years older than him? Ten, fifteen?"

"So? That sort of thing isn't unheard of."

"Charlotte doesn't seem the type."

"It didn't last long." He paused, then looked at his hands. "Not because she's not the type, though. Rob broke it off. She didn't want to. At least that's what he told me."

Jennie stared at Karl. "Does Margaret know?"

"I doubt it. Rob was terrified Margaret would find out, and she's not the type to take that sort of thing lightly. That's why he broke it off. He knew it was a big mistake. From what Rob said, Charlotte didn't agree." He leaned forward. "Don't say anything about this to anyone. Okay? If Margaret didn't know, I'd hate for her to find out now because of me."

"I won't say a word." Jennie thought for a minute. "Did many people at the office know?"

He shrugged. "Enough about that. How about that dinner? Not because I told you about Rob and Charlotte, but because it would be fun. Besides, you owe me a date. You stood me up last time."

"I can't even think about dates until after tonight."

"May I come? Watch the fireworks with you?"

"You can come, but I'll be too busy to pay any attention to you."

"So, I'll be here, but I'll call you tomorrow morning, and we'll make plans." He rose and made a sweeping bow. "Until later, milady."

It wasn't until after he was gone that Jennie remembered she didn't even know where he'd put the fireworks. Oh, well. As Alice had pointed out, it wasn't her problem.

Chapter Twenty-seven

"Come in." The click of knitting needles punctuated Tess's words.

Jennie entered and closed the door behind her.

After a sharp look at Jennie, Tess set her knitting aside. "What happened?"

"This gets more and more complicated." Jennie stared at the cardinal on the windowsill and weighed how much she should confide in Tess. She said, "I know I shouldn't burden you with this, but—"

"We've been through that. You obviously need to talk things out. So . . . spill it." Tess pronounced the last two words like a character from an old noir crime film and mimed puffing a cigarette, then blowing smoke from a corner of her mouth.

Humor seemed to put a more manageable perspective on the past twenty-four hours. Jennie laughed, then swore Tess to secrecy and told her about Preston's disappearance, the break-in at her house, and the little bombshell Karl had just dropped. "That puts things into a different light, don't you think?"

"You mean the Rob and Charlotte fling?"

"Yes. I thought all along money was the reason, and, much as I didn't want to believe it, Web seemed the most likely person, especially since the money showed up in his account. Now . . . maybe Charlotte had another reason. Of course, even if money is the motive, you have to wonder about her."

"Because of her interest in investment property?"

"Yes. I still think that may be key. If she needed money right away, like for a down payment, she might have taken the funds, thinking she could replace them before anybody discovered they were missing. Then something went wrong. Rob found out, and she ended up killing him. She seems to be only so-so with computers, but Karl says it's an act. That's always been in the back of my mind as possible, but . . ." She hesitated, thinking for a minute. "Why would she put the money into Web's account? What good would that do her?"

Tess nodded, encouraging Jennie to continue.

"Another possibility . . . maybe Margaret Payton found out about Charlotte and Rob."

Tess asked, "Did Karl say when the incident occurred?"

"Last summer, so about a year ago. He said Margaret's not the type to take something like that lightly. Maybe she killed her husband and set the whole thing up. She's plenty smart. That's obvious when you talk to her." Jennie rooted in her purse until she found the paper she was looking for. She handed it to Tess. "Here's a list of names Margaret made for me. People she wanted me to talk to." Jennie glanced at the list. "Charlotte's name is first." She looked up at Tess. "Karl said Margaret didn't know, but . . . what do you think?"

"She probably at least suspected. You said she's not dumb."

"No, definitely not. What can you tell from her handwriting?"

Tess looked at the paper, then at Jennie. "When did Margaret write this?"

"It was"—Jennie had to stop and think, so much had happened in the past few days—"Monday afternoon."

"So it was after her husband's death?"

"Yes, right after."

Tess shook her head. "Every stroke indicates confusion and anger, but that's to be expected."

Jennie anticipated where Tess was going. "You're saying anybody whose husband was just murdered might write like that?"

"Maybe not exactly like this, but their writing would show a troubled state of mind. The question is, why was she troubled? I can't answer that. Graphology has its limitations." She removed her glasses and dangled them over the chair arm as she looked at Jennie. "Your instincts have to help you here. If you had to guess, what would your guess be?"

Jennie spoke softly, as much to herself as Tess. "Margaret was upset because her husband had just been murdered, and it was a complete shock. She'd worried about his going to the bank to meet Preston but hadn't expected anything this bad. And she blamed herself for not trying harder to stop him." She stopped and thought for a minute longer. "Or, maybe she killed him because she found out about him and Charlotte. And she's in shock because she didn't realize she was capable of murder. Plus, she's scared. She doesn't know if she can get away with it. That would explain something else—her reason for calling me. She wanted to know what I saw."

Tess watched Jennie with a proud half smile. "Two very good guesses. Both logical. But are they correct? Any other ideas?"

"Charlotte. I need to think about Charlotte Ellio. It was probably her earring at my house. Does that mean she was there? Or just that someone wanted it to look as if she was? That could lead back to Margaret, if she knew about the so-called fling. What if she found the earring in her husband's pocket, and that's how she found out? When I talked to Charlotte, she seemed to think Web had done both the murder and funds transfer. But if she was guilty, that's what she'd say, because she set it up by using Web's computer to transfer the money. That would be so stupid. I can't believe she'd think she could get away with it." Jennie rubbed her forehead, as though trying to smooth her thoughts. "One thing I'm sure of. Charlotte doesn't like Web." She rose from the chair, unable to remain seated any longer. "That still leaves Preston. Why did he leave? One thing I know for sure is that he's the one who talked me into going to the bank that night. So he had to know something was wrong." She looked at Tess. "Right?"

Tess didn't say anything, but she had that *Mona Lisa* smile again.

Jennie paced the distance between the chairs and door until she forced her thoughts into a semblance of order. "Okay, here's how I see it. I can't do anything about Preston right now, so I won't worry about him. I'm going to call both Margaret and Charlotte and see if I can get them to talk to me again." She looked at Tess's clock. "I can't do it now because I have to meet Masoski at my house at one. That might be good. Maybe after I talk to him, I'll have a better idea which one it is." She started to leave, then thought of something else. "Remember the text message?"

"The one you said wasn't a threat?"

Jennie nodded. "I found out it was made from Charlotte's phone, but that doesn't mean a thing. I saw the phone lying on her desk, where anyone could pick it up and use it."

"Did you tell the police?"

"Yes, but I can't really say it was a threat."

Tess said, "Any anonymous message should be considered a threat. Be careful."

"I will," Jennie said, but her mind was already too far away to think about the warning or the years of experience that had prompted it.

Chapter Twenty-eight

Masoski was waiting in his car when Jennie pulled into her drive. She glanced at the phone on the seat beside her, considering leaving it there. She still hadn't heard from Leda but didn't want to talk to her in front of the lieutenant. She put the phone on vibrate and slipped it into a pocket.

They entered the house together. Masoski surveyed the chaos of the family room through narrowed eyes.

Jennie asked, "Learn anything?"

He answered her question with a request. "Tell me again what Preston Barrons said when you made the arrangements for you to go to the bank Sunday night."

She did her best to remember his instructions.

Masoski closed his eyes as he listened. When she'd finished, he opened them and asked, "Two o'clock. You sure of the time?"

"Positive."

"Margaret Payton said her husband was supposed to meet Barrons at midnight."

"I know. I don't understand the time difference either."

His eyes held Jennie's in an unblinking gaze. "You don't have to understand. Nothing makes my job harder than an amateur Sherlock Holmes."

She didn't bother to comment on that.

He said, "You didn't tell me everything last night."

"What do you mean?"

"Where are Preston Barrons and his son?" He uprighted the wing chair and sat in it.

"Why would I know that? And why would I mention it to you if I did?"

Masoski spoke slowly, pausing after each statement as if he were addressing a backward six-year-old. "Last night you and Mrs. Barrons were together. I've never had the impression you were best friends. Yet you were here together, going to a movie, coming back to your house, apparently to spend the night." There came an especially long pause. "And we have another crime. Every time something happens, it involves you and someone from that family." He leaned forward. "Coincidence?"

"Well—"

They both jumped when the doorbell rang.

Masoski looked at Jennie. "Expecting anyone?"

"No." She stood where she was until he inclined his head toward the front hall.

She opened the door to Brooke Newton, notepad in hand, a smirk on her face. "I told you I'd be back. I didn't think it would be here, though." She waved the notepad and came inside without waiting for an invitation. "Whoo!" She took in the disheveled family room. "I heard you were broken into, but . . . looks like somebody was seriously looking for something." She turned to Masoski. "Know who did this?"

He hunched his shoulders, didn't speak.

Brooke tried again. "Did you find out who the earring belongs to?"

He came out of the chair like a shot and bounded over to Jennie. "I told you not to mention the earring."

"I didn't."

He spun to face Brooke. "How do you know about it?" He took three steps and loomed over her, scowling.

She didn't back down. "News of the burglary came in over the radio. I was assigned to cover it."

"The earring? Was that on the radio?"

No answer.

"How'd you find out about it?"

"I can't tell you that. My sources—"

"*Sources.* That old song and dance." He did a surprisingly graceful dance step, then smiled at Brooke. "If I tell you about the earring, will you name your sources?"

Brooke's eyes widened. She seemed to consider, then finally said, "I can't do that."

The next thirty seconds felt like the pause in a child's tantrum.

Brooke spoke first. "How about Preston Barrons? Does anyone know where he is?"

Masoski asked, "Who told you about that?"

"It's common knowledge."

"How common?"

"Pretty much all over Memphis."

Both Brooke and Masoski looked at Jennie.

She shrugged and, when they continued to stare, resisted the impulse to fill the silence.

Masoski faced Brooke. "Mrs. Connors is not prepared to give out information. You have more questions for me?"

A vibration against Jennie's hip distracted her and kept her from hearing all of Brooke's answer. She refocused in time to hear Brooke ask, "When's the big fireworks display?"

She realized that question was for her. "Tonight. Starts at dusk."

"Visitors welcome?"

"Sure."

Brooke smiled. "Maybe I'll come. It should be interesting." She imitated Masoski's dance step and departed with a jaunty wave.

Masoski remained motionless until they heard Brooke's engine start. Then he sat down again and said, "You have anything else to tell me?"

"No."

He gestured toward the scattered papers. "Any idea what they were looking for?"

"No. And I don't know if anything's missing. Won't until I go through things. Maybe not even then."

He looked around the room again. "You're not staying here tonight?"

"I haven't thought that far ahead. I have to get back to Riverview. Fourth of July's a big deal for our residents, and they're depending on me to take care of the details. We about finished here?"

He was quiet—he seemed to be thinking—and finally said, "Yeah. I'd advise you to find another place to stay until we have some answers."

"Okay."

Jennie watched him leave, then checked her phone. There was a message from Leda: "They called. They're coming home." She tried to call Leda but was unable to get through to her on the cell, so she tried the house.

Dorothea Samson answered.

"Hi, it's Jennie. May I speak to Leda?"

"If you'd like to leave a message, I'll give it to her."

Jennie knew better than to try to get past Dorothea when she used that tone. She said, "Just tell her I called." After she hung up, she looked around, debated starting the cleanup, then decided it wasn't the highest priority. Dare she risk a shower? She told herself the burglar would wait to make sure the cop wasn't coming back. And she needed that shower. She locked all the doors and headed for the bathroom.

Five minutes later, with steam rising about her, she reflected on the two telephone calls she'd planned to make as soon as Masoski left. No time now. Besides, why make two calls when one would do? The exchange between Masoski and Brooke had given her a pretty good idea of whom she needed to talk to. Should she have shared that with the lieutenant? No, not until she had something concrete to back it up. Besides, she had to get to Riverview as soon as possible.

Fireworks awaited.

Chapter Twenty-nine

It was almost four by the time Jennie reached Riverview. She considered going by Tess's room to fill her in, but there was too much to be done for tonight. She found Alice on the front lawn, supervising the setup of chairs. Karl was there, too, helping. He waved and flashed that smile when he saw Jennie.

She went over to him. "I'm surprised you actually came."

Alice overheard. "He came looking for you, and, believe me, he's been a godsend."

Another smile from Karl. "Yep. I rode up on a white horse. Parked him out back."

"Hope you plan to clean up after him."

Alice took offense on his behalf. She waved to the chairs. "He set up most of these." She faced Jennie, hands on hips. "Which is very nice, considering it's your responsibility, and you keep disappearing."

Jennie kept her cool—with an effort. "My house was

broken into last night. I had to meet Lieutenant Masoski there this afternoon."

Alice deflated. "You could have let me know."

Jennie didn't bother to answer.

Alice went on, still praising Karl. "He even helped the workmen move the fireworks out to the island." She aligned two chairs that were ruining the symmetry of her row. "I'll admit you were right about one thing. The men who delivered the fireworks were totally disorganized. Didn't even know how many boxes they'd brought. They accused us of losing one. I told them to check their invoice."

Jennie asked, "Did they find the box?"

"I guess. They didn't bother me again." She squinted down the row of chairs, then looked at Jennie. "Think you can finish this? I have other things to see to."

"Sure," Jennie said.

When they were alone, Karl asked, "How'd the meeting go? Did they catch the burglar?"

"Not yet." After a few minutes during which they worked side by side, placing chairs in rows facing out toward the island, Jennie asked, "Has your boss come back?"

He shrugged.

Jennie said, "Brooke Newton showed up at the house while I was there with Masoski. Apparently rumors are flying all over town."

"The Barronses aren't going to be happy about that."

Jennie sat in the chair she'd just placed. "What prompted Preston to leave in the first place?"

"How would I know?"

"You didn't say anything to make him think Web had made the transfer and killed Rob to cover up?"

"Me? You kidding?" His blue eyes were as wide and innocent as a newborn's.

Jennie persisted. "Did you?"

He sat beside her and tried to take her hand. "You really think I'd do that?"

She didn't answer.

"Okay. I'll level with you. I didn't, but I know who did."

"What do you mean?"

He stood. "Come with me."

"First tell me who."

"You haven't figured it out? Charlotte. Who else?"

Jennie just looked at him.

He stared back. "I have proof."

"I'll believe it when I see it."

"I told Alice I was looking for you. Actually, I came looking for Lieutenant Masoski. When he wasn't here, I figured he would be sooner or later."

"What about the proof?"

"I left it inside . . . to show him when he gets here. But I can trust you. Come on."

Jennie couldn't play the game any longer. She blurted it out. "Stop lying. I know you killed Rob."

He appeared sad but unshaken. "Me?"

Jennie called his bluff, wondering just how far he'd go before he admitted the truth. "Show me this proof."

"Sure." He headed for Riverview's front door.

She hesitated, then followed him across the lawn and into the building, telling herself she was safe with so many people around.

He led her to a door and pushed it open.

The room was one the architect had stuck in under the

eaves in an effort to use every inch of space. It had looked good on the blueprint but, in reality, was too small and out of the way for any real use. Eventually they'd bricked over the outside door, and occasionally someone thought to use the space for storage.

Jennie remained an arm's length away. "How did you know about this room?"

"Alice showed it to me. This is where we put the fireworks. I figured it would be a good place to leave my evidence, since she said no one ever uses it."

Jennie peered into the darkness. A hand on her back propelled her the rest of the way in. She heard the door close. The darkness became complete. She tried to turn, but the hand moved from her back to around her waist. She fought to remain calm. "You won't get away with it." She opened her mouth to scream.

His other hand shot up; his fingers clamped her jaw wide, silencing her. He hissed into her ear, "Listen to me."

She tried to get her teeth around his fingers.

He squeezed, harder, until she felt as if her jaw would crack. The fingers of the his hand closed around her bad wrist and pulled it behind her.

The pain made her light-headed, but she used her free hand to grab his hair.

He shook her off, spun her around, and pushed her against a wall. Both of her arms were pinned behind her. He kept one hand over her mouth. "Okay. I killed Rob, but I had every reason. If you'll listen, you'll understand."

She twisted her body and tried to free her hands, but he was too strong.

"Rob set the whole thing up. Nobody was supposed to get hurt. It was his idea to transfer the money into Web's account." He seemed compelled to explain, almost as if that would make what he had done okay.

Jennie stopped struggling. *If I play along, maybe he'll let me go.*

Karl went on. "Since I know computers, he talked me into doing it for him. He arranged the meeting with Preston. Said he'd prove to Preston that his kid took the money, then let Preston talk him out of going to the police. I'd cover it up, make the whole thing look like a computer glitch. The money would be back where it belonged. We'd both be heroes. Be promoted, get big raises. Nobody would be hurt." His eyes glittered in the dark.

Karl kept his hold on her. "That's what Rob said. We went to the bank at midnight. Rob had me show him all the computer manipulations. Then I found out he was going to double-cross me. He got Preston's gun and tried to take me prisoner. When Preston showed up at two, instead of proving to Preston that Web took the money, he was going to tell him I'd made the transfer. His story made sense. I'm the IT guy. Rob would be the hero. I'd be the patsy." There was a hollow laugh. "Well, I quashed that. I got the gun away from him." He moved away slightly without removing his hand from Jennie's mouth. "But I didn't mean to kill him. It was his fault. Just like this is your fault." He leaned into her.

She was flattened against the wall, with Karl's fingers crushing her jaw.

His other hand came up, replacing the one over Jennie's face.

She smelled something. Ether.

Chapter Thirty

Consciousness came slowly. Jennie lay on her side, with her head jammed against a hard surface, her neck bent into an awkward angle. Her tongue hurt. Something pressed it down. The sides of her mouth were stretched open. Her throat felt as if someone had taken a file to it. She attempted a deep breath but choked. She tried to sit up. Her body refused.

She lay still, remembering: the scent of ether; the desperate attempt to hold her breath; Karl's fingers like an iron clamp on her face; and, most of all, the catlike quickness with which he had pushed her into the small space. How could she have underestimated him so? She told herself it did no good to think about that. *Concentrate on now.* Her arms and legs were stretched behind her, tied together. That wasn't hard to figure out. Something was stuffed into her mouth and secured by a band around her head. The band's edges were stiff and grated against her cheeks—likely an old paint rag somebody had tossed onto the floor. Turpentine-scented fumes wafted around her. Another smell. It took her a minute to place the second odor—sulfur.

She scooted over the floor, testing her limbs and muscles. Nothing was broken. Her knee struck something, not soft but less hard than the floor and walls. She twisted until her fingertips touched the object. They slipped upward in a straight line and found a corner. *A box.* She focused on that, the one small detail of her surroundings she recognized. The sulfur odor was stronger beside the box. *The missing box of fireworks?*

As her head cleared, she listened to sounds outside the dark, cramped space. Voices, diffused by distance, reached her. She knew she was in the little-used storeroom. Riverview's main entry was just down the hall. How far? She visualized the building's layout, doing a mental room count to calculate the distance. Fifty feet was her best guess. She heard the front door open, close, open again, voices, footsteps. So close. She tried to cry out. Impossible. She banged her knees against the floor, then stopped and listened for a sign that someone had heard. Nothing.

A familiar squeak told her that someone was setting the iron bar that held the front door open. She heard shuffles and murmuring voices. *Everyone's going outside.* She ran through the schedule she'd worked out so carefully. *So they've eaten. Time for the band concert.*

She heard instruments warming up, a long pause, and the strains of the national anthem. She imagined the veterans standing as tall as their arthritis would allow, with their hands in salutes or over their hearts. For the first time, tears threatened. *Stop! You don't have time for this. Think!*

A lone pair of footsteps approached and stopped nearby. The next sound was a faint scratching, followed by a click. A shaft of blinding light forced her eyes shut. The door closed softly. When she opened her eyes again, the light was gone, but there was an undeniable presence in the space with her.

She lay still and felt as much as heard him approach. She knew he was standing over her. His clothing rustled when he moved. A shadow, denser than the other darkness, leaned close. She felt his fingers on her wrists, then her ankles, and she knew he was testing the knots.

"This is your own fault, you know." He spoke in a whisper. His breath touched her face. Peppermint mingled with the odor of turpentine. He knelt beside her. "I really like you. If only I could trust . . ."

"Argh."

"You want to say something? Sorry. If I knew you wouldn't scream . . ." He sounded so reasonable. His clothes rustled again. A beam of light hit her in the face.

What's he doing? She watched him place a cylinder—a flashlight—on the frame of the transom above the bricked-over door and remove something from his pocket. Then something else.

A candle?

He struck a match, lit the candle, and set it on top of the box. He shone the flashlight over the arrangement, nodded, turned off the flashlight, and jammed it into his pocket. He looked down and nudged Jennie with his toe. "You want to know what's going to happen, don't you?"

His breath sent the candle's flame into a flickering dance. Its light distorted his features and erased all likeness to the handsome man who had so captivated her. This time she didn't try to speak. "I guess you have that right." He pointed to the candle. "When that burns down, the box will ignite, and you"— long pause—"will go up in a blaze of glory." He sounded supremely satisfied, insanely calm. "And I'll be outside, enjoying the show. When it's over, they'll find evidence. All pointing to Charlotte." He leaned closer. "Her own fault. She shouldn't leave her phone and earrings lying around. She's here. Summoned by a message from you. Relayed by me."

Jennie lurched, almost scoring a head-butt to his midsection.

He dodged and continued without a break. "Of course, Charlotte will insist I told her you invited her. Since you won't be here, it'll be my word against hers. And, with the evidence . . ." He went to the door, paused, then turned to look at Jennie. His smile was sadly sweet. "I wish it didn't have to end like this."

She watched him, trying to reconcile his benign demeanor with his deadly intent. Even now, when he was about to kill her, there was no hint of the psychopath in his perfect features. How could that be? Had there been signs along the way that she'd missed? Now that she knew the truth, it was easy to see his hand behind so many things. He must have been the source Brooke had refused to name. It wasn't hard to picture him charming the young reporter, feeding her information and prompting her to ask the questions he wanted answered, all the while remaining a safe distance from the police. *That was smart. Masoski would've seen through him. That story he fed me about Charlotte and Rob, To think I believed him!* Yes, Karl was smart, charming, and handsome but completely without conscience. Finally, Jennie thought she understood. A person with no conscience doesn't feel guilt, so they don't act guilty.

He was still standing there, his ear against the door, apparently listening. Then he opened the door and slipped through.

Jennie was alone again but no longer in darkness—a mixed blessing. The candle that relieved her fear added to her danger. She knew that and still, against all reason, welcomed the light.

More patriotic music reached her. "Stars and Stripes Forever." She heard nothing to indicate there was anyone else in the building. *It's up to me.* She kept moving her hands. She hoped the knots would shift and create slack in the loop around her wrists. Eventually she'd be able to slip her hands through. *Eventually.* She glanced at the candle's flame and twisted her hands. The pain of her injured wrist forced her legs out in an involuntary kick. She pictured Tommy and Andy's faces, steeled herself against the pain, and kept rotating her hands. She stopped for a second. The loop seemed . . . not loose but less tight.

There were sounds in the hall.

"Jennie?" There could be no mistaking Nate's sonorous tones. He was close.

Jennie thumped her elbows against the box. The candle swayed, threatening to topple. *Jeez!* She moved away, banging on the floor with her elbows.

"Jennie?" The disembodied voice moved away.

Then a different accent, pitched higher, called her name.

She kept moving her hands in quarter, then half, rotations, as Tess's voice came closer. She hit the floor with her elbow again. Tess's voice faded.

She fought her rising panic. *They'll be back. If I can get my hands free by then . . .* She held that thought and continued to work her hands. The loop felt looser. She tried to slip one hand through. *Not yet. But soon.* Against her will, she looked at the shrinking candle. *Just a little more.* The candle sputtered. She jerked and felt the rope give. She brought her hands together and squeezed her fingers through. Her hands were free. There was half an inch of candle left. She tore the gag from her mouth and gulped the air. She crawled to the door and tried the knob. Locked. She banged on it with both fists. "I'm in the storeroom!" She paused, hearing footsteps. She sat on the floor to untie her legs, screaming, "The storeroom!"

Nate was there first. "Jennie?"

"Yes!" She glanced at the candle. "Hurry!"

"What happened?"

"Never mind that. Get me out."

She heard Tess's voice. "Try the knob."

Then Nate again. "Locked. I'll get the fire ax."

"Get my knitting bag. I'll stay here with her."

Jennie looked at the candle, realizing she should move it off the box. She grabbed at the remaining stub. The flame scorched her hand, and she dropped the candle. The wax spread and left a guttering flame that refused to go out. She picked up the gag and tried to extinguish the flame, but the cloth caught fire. *The turpentine!*

The cardboard began to smolder.

Jennie looked toward the bricked-over door, shuddered, and looked farther up. There was a transom above the door with a ledge about ten inches wide. If she could get up there, she could open the window. As she clambered onto the box, she heard clicking sounds at the door. *Tess with her knitting needles.* The top of the box was burning now. "Get away!" she shouted to Tess. *Can't wait.* She used her right arm to hoist herself up, crouched on the ledge, and tried to force the window open with her left hand. The bad wrist sent daggers shooting up to her elbow, but the window refused to budge. She pushed again. More daggers of pain, but the window moved.

Below her, the door trembled. The fire ax blade penetrated the upper panel. Nate and Tess almost had the door open, but the box was collapsing inward, with the flames about to fall into the fireworks.

"Get away!" Jennie shouted again to Tess. She ignored her pain and pushed harder. The window swung up. She dove through. A boxwood broke her fall. She tumbled from the bushes, rolled out onto the lawn, and tried to stand, but her ankle wouldn't support her weight. Behind her, she heard the wooden door splinter.

Nate screamed, "Where is she?"

And Tess's voice, excited but reasonable, said, "The window's open. She got out."

And then, from where Jennie lay in the grass, the world seemed to detonate. Fireworks erupted in the sky across the river. A series of pops mingled with excited oohing and aahing and laughter. A child began to cry. On her other side, flames climbed higher and danced behind the transom window.

Movement near Riverview's front door caught her eye. Nate and Tess rushed out. They looked terrified but were intact.

Jennie had to reassure them. "I'm okay!" she shouted. Then they were standing over her—two dear, familiar faces—and she realized it was true. She tried again to stand.

"Don't get up." Tess's voice was calm.

Nate lowered himself to the grass and grasped Jennie's hand. He said nothing, silent for the first time in her memory.

Tess said, "Stay with her. I'll get help." She turned and almost collided with Lieutenant Masoski.

"What happened?" he asked.

Jennie tried to answer, but her voice was drowned out by more popping sounds. Much closer now. Fireworks spewed from Riverview's ill-fated storeroom. They were so close that she had to turn her head. She saw a tall male figure rise from the chairs and look toward them. "It was Karl!" she screamed, waving frantically at the figure edging through the rows of chairs.

Masoski looked puzzled for a moment, then seemed to understand. He turned and broke into a run.

The tall figure bolted from the chairs and ran down the lawn, looking over his shoulder.

Masoski picked up his pace.

So did Karl. He reached River Road and didn't stop.

Horns blasted. Brakes screeched. Shattering glass competed with exploding fireworks.

A truck fishtailed. The tall figure flew through the air like a rag doll. And landed on the pavement.

Karl Erickson was dead. There was no way he could have survived that.

Jennie watched and felt nothing.

Tess reappeared, with Woody in tow. An aide pushing a gurney followed.

Brooke Newton was right behind them. She darted around them and knelt by Jennie's side. "You okay?"

Jennie nodded, surprised that she'd asked.

Brooke pulled out her notebook. "What happened?"

This was more like it.

Woody pushed the reporter aside and signaled to the aide.

Jennie protested. "It's okay. I need to talk to her."

Woody shook his head. "It can wait."

Every part of Jennie's body hurt as they loaded her onto the gurney and headed for the door. She distracted herself by looking at the sky. Colors filled the darkness like flowers in a giant's garden. *I hope Tom found a fireworks display for the kids.*

Somehow, she was sure that he had.

Chapter Thirty-one

The limo glided to the front entrance of the Peabody Hotel, and the driver scrambled out to open the door for Jennie. A good thing, too. With one arm in a sling and one leg in a cast, she needed help to navigate the short stretch of sidewalk and, even more, to manipulate the crutch through the revolving door.

Inside, an impeccably groomed young woman appeared at Jennie's side. A brass pin above her pocket gave her name as Nancy Ames. She told the driver, "I'll take over now." To Jennie, she said, "Everyone else is here. They're waiting upstairs."

Jennie paused at the fountain to watch the ducks. They quacked and squabbled in their small pool, but would any of them kill for a better position? She doubted it.

What is it about the human race?

Going up in the elevator, Jennie had a few minutes alone to reflect on the week since Riverview's fire and

262

her own too-close encounter with fireworks. None of the residents' rooms had been damaged, but the front of the building, where the administrative offices were lodged, had taken a major hit. That was unfortunate, but Jennie was glad that none of the residents had been hurt.

She felt good, too, about the article Brooke Newton had written. Not only was Riverview Manor portrayed in glowing terms, but Charlotte Ellio was cleared of any wrongdoing. After a few phone calls, Jennie had learned that other employees had seen Karl in Charlotte's office when she wasn't there. It wasn't hard to convince Masoski that Karl had used Charlotte's cell phone to leave the warning text message for Jennie and had stolen an earring to plant at the scene when he searched her house. All in all, things had worked out pretty well.

The one thing Jennie could not feel good about was how Rob Payton's involvement would affect his widow and daughter.

Preston, Leda, and Webster Barrons, along with Hamilton Sunderson, were seated at a long table with large, curling pieces of paper in front of them.

The men rose when Jennie came in.

Preston pulled out a chair for her.

She remained standing, faced Preston, and asked, "What's going to happen to Margaret Payton?" No use beating around the bush.

A muscle twitched in Preston's cheek.

She forged ahead anyway. "How will she and Chloe manage? Financially, I mean." When he didn't answer, she said, "You'll make sure she gets the money from her husband's pension plan and anything else he had coming, won't you?" She paused and added, "I'd consider it a personal favor."

Preston glanced at Sunderson.

Leda cleared her throat, making her presence felt.

Web said, "Please, Dad."

Preston nodded. "I'll take care of it."

Jennie sat down next to Leda and pointed to the drawings. "Are these the plans for the reconstruction?"

Leda said, "We'll get to that. We have something else to discuss first."

"Oh?"

"How would you like to be Assistant Director of Riverview Manor?"

Jennie was taken off guard.

Leda added, "It would mean quite a bit more money."

Jennie stalled. How could she say no to that? "Would I still get to work with the residents?" If not, how could she say yes?

Leda adjusted her glasses in that familiar way. "You'd be working directly with me, making important decisions that influence Riverview's future."

"I'm not so sure," Jennie said, "that planning the future is more important than making people happy day to day. That's what I'm good at, and I love it."

Leda didn't answer.

Jennie went on, "But I think it's worth more than I'm getting paid now"—she smiled broadly—"especially the past couple of weeks."

"About that . . ." Leda pushed a check across the table.

Jennie gasped when she saw the amount. She knew to the penny how much she had coming. She hadn't expected a bonus, certainly not one of this magnitude. She managed to stammer, "Thanks."

"You earned it," Leda said. "Think about my offer. I'm sure we can work out a compromise."

Jennie thought so, too. She didn't know what the future held for Riverview, but she knew she wanted to have a hand in shaping it.